THE WARM UP

XIO AXELROD

XIO AXELROD

For Mr. X, who knows how lucky he was to marry a hockey chick; for Teemu Selanne, my hockey boyfriend; and for Eric Desjardins, whose grace, speed, and intelligence on the ice ignited my love for the sport. Let's go Flyers, let's go!

FOREWORD

THE WARM UP was originally part of *Hot On Ice: a Hockey Romance Anthology*, a short-lived collection of stories published in March 2017. This edition contains bonus material. Enjoy!

PROLOGUE

IN CONSTANTINE ZIMIN'S twenty-seven years on planet earth, nothing had ever tasted so bittersweet.

The Cup - THE motherfucking Cup - was right there at center ice, surrounded by hockey legends, the league's commissioner, and some other people he honestly didn't recognize, so screw 'em. Soon, Zim and the New Orleans Cajun Rage would be announced as the 2016 Cup Champions.

He felt under his jersey for the thick, silver chain he knew would be there, and brought it to his lips, kissing it with a silent word. *Mila.*

His twin sister would have been there to cheer him on. Should have been. Ten years after they'd lost her, the pain had never been so acute as it was at that moment. She had always been his number one cheerleader, even before his parents. Not a day went by that he didn't miss her.

"This is fucking unreal!" The Rage's starting goalie, Flynn Kazakov, yelled, champing at the bit to get his hands on the trophy. "Can you believe this?"

"I know!" Zim shouted over the cacophony, a mixture of cheering fans, and booming announcements.

Flynn clapped him hard on the shoulder, laughing. "Soak it in, my man! Soak it in."

Zim knew how much it meant to the guy. It was the same for all of them. Though each man had his reasons, his own personal demons that he'd had to fight to get to this point in his life, they were all there to share in the glory of this success.

All but one.

Zim's best friend, his teammate for nearly as many years as he'd been in pro hockey, Jonas Magnusson, was not beside him. He hadn't been there for the thrilling final game. He wasn't there to hoist The Cup over his head and take a lap around the ice. He wouldn't be back in the locker room to guzzle champagne from its gleaming, silver bowl.

Instead, Jonas was laid up in a hospital bed with a concussion and a goddamned broken leg because he – Zim – hadn't been on the ice to protect him.

So, yeah. This was as fucking bittersweet as it came. No Mila. No Jonas. Not even his parents could make it out for this final game.

He thought about calling Jonas from the ice, getting the asshole on the phone and letting him hear the deafening cheers from their home crowd. Maybe he was watching on television, though Zim doubted it. The guy had been so out of it when he'd dropped by earlier in the day.

Fuck.

"You look like you stepped in shit," yelled rightwinger, Ransom Cox. Right in Zim's motherfucking ear. "We just won The Cup, man! There'll be bunnies lined up for days after this."

Zim nodded and forced a smile. It wasn't like Coxy to drown himself in puck bunnies, but it was a special occasion.

"Fucking unreal, ain't it?"

Ransom nodded, grinning like an idiot.

Zim had to laugh.

Jonas and Mila would both kick his ass if he didn't enjoy this moment, so he concentrated on doing just that. The truth was, other than his parents and Magnussen, Zim didn't have anyone to share this with after the lights dimmed and the parties ended. It was a sobering thought, and he wasn't even drunk yet.

This should have felt bigger, like the culmination of something. Instead, it seemed more like the means to an end.

Ladies and gentlemen, your 2016 Cup Champion Cajun Rage!

The arena exploded with riotous cheers and applause while their fight song blared from every speaker.

Zim had waited his whole life for this moment. Had shed buckets of blood, and oceans of sweat and tears for it. He'd protected their lead in game seven with a fortunate kick save, helping out their goalie and securing the team's place in history. Zim had earned this. He should have been over the fucking moon, but it rang hollow.

Tonight, he'd celebrate with his teammates and then head over to sit with Jonas. He had to wake up soon, right? The fucker had better.

Zim would make sure Jonas was okay, and then he'd take his $200,000 bonus and head back home to Philly for the summer. Get things rolling on a project he'd been wanting to do for a long, long time. Something he'd been wanting to do for Mila, in her memory.

"Zimmer!" Rightwinger Archie Durham yelled for Zim, and he realized Archer had The Cup in his hands. Archers grinned widely as he skated toward him. "Time for a spin around the ice by the man who saved our collective asses."

Zim had a plan, a promise he'd made to himself years ago. After tonight, he'd be going home as a champion. He just might have the means to make that promise a reality. It was something. This moment was something.

He hoisted The Cup over his head, and then he took that goddamned lap.

CHAPTER 1

Suji,

I'm sorry to do this in a letter. It's shitty, I know, but you know what a coward I am. Neither of us ever really felt like it was working, so me leaving without saying goodbye face-to-face shouldn't be a shock.

Listen, I'll never forget you. You're loyal, and your devotion to the hospital is great, but I realized I need more. My career's taking off, and I need someone by my side. I know you live for your work, and I should have been more understanding, but we are who we are. You taught me that.

Deep down, I think you knew it was over, but you hung in there anyway. Honestly, I don't believe you would have ever walked away. I'm ripping off the bandage.

Find that person – the one who wants to change the world, like you do. Good luck.

All my best,

Brian

Sujarta Meriwether read the letter for the umpteenth time. By now, it was wrinkled, worn in spots, and showing traces of dried tears where the ink had smudged.

After three months, she had no more tears for that failed relationship. The only evidence that she and Brian had ever lived together sat patiently at her feet, waiting for her to acknowledge it.

She patted the space next to her on the plastic-covered couch and Jasmine, her white Persian cat, jumped up and settled at her side. Absentmindedly, Suji stroked the animal. The tactile memories brought on by such a simple act would probably always assault her, she mused.

Running from the car with Brian, in the pouring rain, to the house with the sign in the yard that read *Free Kittens*.

Bringing a five-week-old Jasmine to their new home and play-arguing over her name.

Spending an obscene amount of money at PetWorld to make Jasmine's little corner of the living room a cat haven.

Nearly four years later, surrounded by moving boxes and the smell of fresh paint, Suji looked around at the skeletal remains of what she once thought would be the rest of her life with Brian, and tried to name the emotion she felt.

"Empty," she said to Jasmine as she got up and got back to work.

Jasmine only yawned.

"Suji?"

"Back here, Amri."

"Jesus. How did I not know you were a hoarder?" Suji's sister, Amrita, worked her slender, five-foot-eleven-inch frame through the maze of stacked boxes and into the spare bedroom. She stopped in the doorway, shaking her head.

Suji touched-up the paint around the window trim. "What?"

"Why are you doing that?" Amrita ambled over to her.

"I want my security deposit back."

"Suji, this place is immaculate. You'd think no one ever lived here at all, much less two people and…" She picked a clump of white hair off her black t-shirt. "A molting cat."

She brushed her hands on her jeans.

They both watched as the clump fell to the hardwood floor and Amrita slid it to the side with the toe of her sandal. She started to run a hand over her thick, dark chocolate hair but seemed to change her mind at the last second, using the inside of her forearm instead.

Suji stood from her crouching position and took in the state of the room. "Yeah, I guess it is pretty spic-and-span, aside from a few furballs."

It was much like the rest of the two-bedroom apartment, crisp and clean, aside from the multitude of boxes and bags awaiting the movers. She placed her brush into the small can of white touch-up paint and removed her gloves, tossing them onto the protective plastic covering the floor.

The sun poured in through the bay window, catching Amrita in a pool of light. Her tawny skin and dark, cinnamon hair framed by gold.

Suji found herself staring at her sister. She'd always thought of herself as attractive enough, but at that moment she felt like a sack of potatoes standing in the same room as Amrita.

"Do I work too much?"

Amri burst into laughter.

"What's so funny?"

"Wait, were you asking a serious question?" Amri wiped her eyes and caught her breath.

"I think you just answered it." Suji sighed. "No wonder Brian left."

"Oh, fuck that noise," Amri snapped. "I don't want to hear another word about that asshole."

"He wanted to spend more time with me, but since I took over as Head Nurse, I haven't had a lot of free time."

"Hey, I know. But Brian wanted a little woman by his side, not someone with a career," Amrita assured her. "You've always been super driven. It's why you are where you are at thirty-years-old."

"Yeah, but…"

"Nope! No buts."

"Okay," Suji acquiesced. "Okay."

"Are things still crazy in Pediatrics?"

Suji sighed. "The budget cuts are ridiculous. We're using outdated equipment, and the ward is often over-crowded. I'm lucky I have a great staff, and the Head of Pediatrics understands what we're dealing with, but if we don't get a fresh infusion of grant money or a major donor, we're going to have to start turning away patients."

Amri frowned. "But I thought you guys became solvent when the university bought the hospital."

Suji snorted. "It helped, but not enough. There's supposed to be some big, new initiative announced soon. Oh, and while I was out on vacation, they schedule some pro athlete to come in and do a photo op. I think they hope it'll drum up some new donors."

"By the tone of your voice and that sour puss face, I guess you're not a big fan of this idea."

Suji's skin prickled with renewed agitation. She'd nearly gone over to the hospital to rip someone a new one when she got a voicemail telling her the event had been scheduled behind her back. Okay, technically, it wasn't her ward, it was the department head's. And Dr. Calvin Morris was excellent at his job, in addition to being a wonderful pediatrician.

No, Suji didn't have a problem with her boss, other than the fact that he'd agreed to host this sports carnival, subjecting her...*their*...patients to who knows what kind of exploitative exposure.

Well, not on her watch.

"I go back to work tomorrow, and I'm going to put a stop to it."

"I thought the department needed the money," Amrita so helpfully pointed out.

Suji shook her head. "Not this badly, not enough to exploit the kids."

"You're making a pretty big assumption, there."

"Better safe than sorry."

Amri shrugged. "Okay. I get it, and the kids are lucky to have you. Hell, we're all lucky to have you. Fuck Brian's saggy-jeans-ass."

Suji barked out a laugh.

"*Have I told...you lately that I love you,*" she sang using her best Rod Stewart voice as she sauntered over to her sister.

Amrita threw her a look of amused disbelief.

"*Have I told you...there's no one else...above you.*" Suji grabbed her and pulled her into an awkward slow dance.

"You, my dear sister, are one sick puppy."

Suji let her go, laughing. "You know you love it."

She grabbed a marker and a stack of labels and began marking the boxes.

To her surprise, Amrita did the same without Suji having to beg. Amri and manual labor of any kind mixed like oil and water.

"Is any of this stuff Brian's?" Amri smoothed an air bubble out of one label marked DVDs.

"Please. No." Suji exhaled. "There'd be three times as many boxes if he were still here." She looked out the window as the moving truck pulled up. "Of course, I wouldn't be moving if he were still here."

Amri sighed. "Su...

"I know. I just...I'm beginning to doubt I'll ever meet Mr. Right."

"Just make sure you steer clear of any more Mr. Wrongs. I hate seeing you like this."

"Brian wasn't Mr. Wrong, Amrita. He was just Mr. Right Now." She laughed mirthlessly. "Or Mr. Right Then."

"Mr. Left, maybe?" Amrita joked.

"I'd settle for Mr. Mover." The sound of a rumbling engine drew Suji's attention back to the window. "And here they come."

"Good," Amri said brightly. "Let's get your stuff over to your new place and then we can head to Skinner's to celebrate."

"Celebrate what?"

Amrita walked over to Suji, a mischievous grin tugging at her plum-stained lips. "It's been three months, big sister. I think it's time to let your hair down. Maybe find a hottie to have some mindless fun with."

She tugged on Suji's scrunchy and the messy bun she had on the top of her head came tumbling down.

"Hey!"

"Look at you." Amrita stepped back and gave her a once-over. "You're letting all of this go to waste, sweetie. Let some hot, young buck get all up in there and work out your kinks."

Suji rolled her eyes. "I don't do one-night-stands, Amri."

She had never been able to adopt the casual attitude toward sex and dating that her sister, and most of their friends, had. Sex for the sake of sex left a bad taste in her mouth, at least in theory. It wasn't something she'd ever actually put into practice. She'd never begrudge any woman from indulging in whatever safe practices she wanted, with however many partners she chose. As for herself…

"That's your problem right there," Amrita argued. "You have such black and white views about relationships. No one's telling you to have a one-night-stand, per se. I'm just suggesting that we go out tonight, have a few drinks with the girls, and see who might be on the menu. You might meet your first fuckbuddy." She grinned.

"Fuckbuddy?"

"Or whatever." Amrita waved it off, averting her eyes.

"Nope. No suggestions of any kind there, Amri." Suji chuckled. "All right. If we finish at a decent time, I'll go."

"Excellent!" Amrita whipped out her phone. "I'll text Joanna and Lovie. May as well make a Friday night of it."

CHAPTER 2

ZIM STEPPED into Skinner's and was immediately impressed by the feel of the place, whisky-soaked and welcoming. He'd never been to Scotland, but the polished brass and gleaming wood made him feel like he was about to get a taste of it. The pub was big, larger than it appeared from the outside. But as large as it was, it was still cozy. A place where someone could find a dark corner to sit in and not be bothered.

"Well, look who finally decided to drop in," said a familiar voice.

"Yo, Cam." Zim accepted a clapping hug from his friend. "How are ya?"

"I'm good, thanks." Camden Skinner, owner of the establishment and an old friend from Zim's college days, smiled and clasped his shoulder. "When I saw you back in July, you said you would come check out my new place."

Zim rubbed the back of his neck. He sucked when it came to social niceties. "Yeah, sorry about not getting over here sooner."

Camden smiled. Sort of. He wasn't an excitable guy, which was one of the reasons they'd gotten along at school. While the rest of the student body seemed to lose its collective mind every weekend attending party after party after binge-drinking party, he and Cam – and Cam's brother, Pierce – had found common ground in simply watching it all play out.

One favorite pastime was to watch drunk assholes stumble across the quad and take bets. Who would fuck whom? Who would pass out on the grass? Who would end up expelled before the end of the semester?

"I'm here now."

"Better late than never," the other man agreed.

Zim followed Camden to the end of the bar, admiring the sheer volume of colorful taps. He took the last stool and picked up the laminated menu.

Camden continued around and through the opening on the side until he stood on the other side. He placed a coaster in from of Zim and then braced his arms on the bar-top.

"So, what do you think?"

"It's nice, Cam. Really." Zim flipped the menu. "Whoa. Especially this big-ass list of what's on tap."

Camden laughed. "You know me. I love my ale. Fancy anything in particular? Or you want me to make a suggestion?"

"Gimme something dark."

"A stout?" Cam was already preparing a pint glass.

"That'll work." Zim nodded. "So, what made you decide to open a pub? Are things slow with Skin?"

Camden and his brother had opened a business a few years back, The Skin Agency. Zim didn't know much about what they did but knew that it brought in quite a bit of money for the both of them.

Cam grunted. "Skin is fine."

Zim arched an eyebrow. He watched as Cam pulled the perfect pint of Belhaven Stout. The creamy head floating over the dark chocolate ale made his mouth water.

"And Pierce?"

"Pierce is Pierce."

Evidently, Cam wasn't in the mood to talk about his brother, and Zim wasn't about to press.

Camden picked up a flat metal object and scraped off some of the foam, leaving the top of the pint perfectly smooth. He set it down in front of Zim, folded his arms, and waited for him to take a sip.

So he did. "Fuck."

The other man smiled, and Zim could almost see teeth. "Aye. S'good, right?"

"Perfect, thanks."

Zim glanced around the pub, noting the nooks and corners filled with darkened booths, velvet-covered benches, and upholstered leather chairs. On the far wall in the back was a dart board. Signs advertising various products lined the walls, brands that Zim assumed were Scottish. He liked the place, it had character. But it was also pretty empty.

"Did you just open for the day?"

"We were slammed for lunch from noon to two, but there won't be anyone in here again until around five when happy hour starts. After that, we'll have a steady crowd until we close at two in the morning."

There were only three or four other people in the bar, which suited Zim just fine. He'd duck out when the crowd started to thicken.

"So, what have you been doing with yerself all summer?" Camden leaned against the back counter.

"Did some work with a youth hockey camp up in the Poconos, and there's a college kid in my neighborhood that I've been working with too." Zim took a sip of his beer, closing his eyes to savor it. "Damn, that's good."

"Thanks," Cam replied. "You think you might coach when you retire?"

"I hadn't thought about it, but I did enjoy working with the kids."

"I bet the youngins' were thrilled to skate with a Cup champion."

Zim shrugged. "I didn't even bring it up. When they did mention it, I made sure they knew it took a hell of a lot of work to get your hands on that trophy."

Camden chuckled. "Oh, I'm sure ye did."

"Meaning?"

The other man straightened. Grabbing a rag from behind the counter, he wiped down the bartop. "You and my nagshead brother, both so focused on your goals you don't stop to appreciate what you've done. What you could do."

"I do appreciate it," Zim argued. "I just don't go around bragging about it. I didn't win the Cup by myself."

"No one said ye did, mate," Cam replied.

He ran a hand through his black hair. It was longer than Zim had remembered and stuck out in all directions.

"Anyway…did you manage to have any fun on your break? You're heading back down for training soon, right?"

"The camp was fun."

"That's not the kind of fun I mean," Cam smirked. "Tell me you at least got laid. I can't imagine the amount of play you can get after winning something like that."

"No comment. But, hey, I get the Cup all to myself in a few days. I could let you borrow it," Zim joked. "Use it for a pussy magnet."

Camden scoffed. "As if I need a fecking trophy for that."

Zim lifted his glass. "Touché."

Camden was a good looking guy, broad and fit. He'd never had any trouble finding women willing to take a walk through the Highlands with him.

"Hey, you mentioned something about starting a foundation? In Mila's memory?"

"Yeah."

"I think that's fantastic, mate. How is it coming together? Do you need anything from me? I have a lot of connections, you know."

"You do, don't you?" Zim eyed him, his mind shifting gears. "I'll be sure to pick your brain about that. But, yeah, things are coming together. I'm trying to get it off the ground before I leave. Eva, my attorney, she's got the legal stuff under control. My job is to talk to the beneficiary."

"Have you chosen one?"

"Yeah, and I have a meeting with them tomorrow before we hold a benefit announcing the venture."

Camden nodded. "Good, good. I'm sure they'll appreciate the help." A commotion at the door drew his attention, and he glanced at his watch. "That'll be five o'clock."

Zim turned to see a group of people stroll in and head to a large booth. Dressed in suits, the mix of men and women were clearly part of the TGIF, after-work crowd.

A tall, blond kid who looked like he was barely twenty-one darted over to them.

"That one," Camden nodded over toward the waiter. "He's as clueless as you are when it comes to the fairer sex."

Zim turned slowly back to him. "Clueless? I'm not fucking clueless, dude, I just...I don't have time for games. Women play games. Hell, men play games too."

"Some games are fun," Camden retorted, his grin wide and downright evil. He leaned in conspiratorially. "Say you go over to that table, right? That redhead's a pretty one. You could go over there, introduce yourself, tell 'em you're friends with the owner. Offer 'em a drink. On you, of course."

"Of course." Zim rolled his eyes.

"Ask what they do - lawyers, by the look of them," Camden said, disdainfully. "They ask what you do, and you tell them." He snapped his fingers. "Instant damp panties, mate."

"Jesus." Zim laughed.

"What?" Camden held his arms wide.

"I don't need tips on how to pick up women, Cam."

"Prove me wrong."

"I am not going over there. Shit, can't a man just enjoy his second pint in peace?"

Camden smiled. "Was that your way of asking for another?"

"It was."

Two pints turned into four and, as the evening went on, the pub filled up. The music got louder. And Zim felt more relaxed than he had in a long time. He ended up in conversation with a fan of Philadelphia's hockey team. Locals were ride-or-die for the men in orange and black, and Zim loved their passion. He'd grown up watching them play and admired the organization.

"I'm just saying," the guy drawled, several pints of St. Andrew's in his belly. His malty breath filled the space between them as they talk-shouted over the noise. "New Orleans got lucky in the conference final. No one expected Phoenix to play as shitty as they did."

"You don't think it's because people underestimated the Rage?"

"Fuck, no," the guy spat. "Bunch of overrated pussies, except for that guy Donnelly. He's fast as fuck. The defense is pretty solid too."

"Yeah," Camden chimed in. "Subzero is a beast."

To Zim's surprise, the guy nodded. "Oh yeah! Dude, we need to get him to Philly. He deserves to play for a real team."

Across the bar, Cam watched the exchange, clearly amused and itching to drop a truth bomb on the Philly fan.

Zim shook his head, grinning. He hadn't enjoyed himself this much in, well, he couldn't remember when. He was about to set the asshole straight about who was a *real* team when a flash of silver caught his eye. Zim looked over the guy's shoulder and...holy damn.

Four gorgeous girls strolled through the door looking like they'd just been cast in a Super Bowl commercial. They were dressed to kill but with all the subtlety of a pretty poison, not the brute force of a sledgehammer. Zim watched, dumbfounded, as they inched their way toward the bar, having completely tuned-out the guy in front of him.

It was a shortest of the women that had him riveted.

Ebony hair cropped just about her shoulders that swayed and bounced with her movements, she had big, bright eyes, and lips that were tailor-made for him to nibble on. She wore a sheer, white shirt over a white tank top of some kind. Camisole? Fuck if he knew, but she looked damn good. Her jeans were dark navy and fit her like a second skin. Her movements were graceful, almost delicate as she followed her friends.

Seriously, all of them were stunning, but he couldn't stop watching her.

"Someone's got your attention," Camden said, leaning forward to follow Zim's line of sight.

Zim pried his gaze away from the woman, now aware that the man he'd been talking to had left. "You know them?"

Camden nodded.

"Who is the one in the white?"

The other man frowned. "Ohhhh no. You best be turning your thoughts elsewhere, Red is spoken for," Camden warned, nodding toward the group of women.

Confused, Zim glanced back at them. The curly redhead was also wearing white. He hadn't even noticed.

"Not her, the brunette."

Camden looked again, just as the blonde in the group waved over to him, a lovely smile on her equally lovely face.

Just what had Philly been putting in the water lately?

"I don't know her, but if she's a friend of Jo's, you're about to meet her."

Zim grabbed Camden's arm. "Don't say anything about who I am."

Cam stopped, frowning. "What?"

"Don't mention who I am or what I do. In fact, don't even call me Zim. Call me...Con."

"Con?"

"Yeah, just roll with it."

"Whatever you say, *Con.*"

"Cam!" The blonde, Jo, stretched over the bar and threw her arms up, wrapping the around Camden's neck. "How are you, babe?"

"Better, now that you're here, lass." He grinned.

Zim tried not to stare at the petite brunette. A difficult task since she kept biting her lip and smoothing her hands down her shapely thighs. Apparently, she wasn't as comfortable as her friend seemed to be.

She looked up, catching his eye.

He flicked his gaze away to someone behind her and tried to keep the blood from rushing to his head. Both of them.

"What'll it be?" Cam grinned at the curvy blonde.

"We're celebrating my friend's new apartment," Jo exclaimed, her blue eyes flashing. She pulled the brunette toward the bar.

The poor girl lost her balance and fell forward.

Without thinking, Zim reached out and caught her before she face-planted in his crotch. Something he almost regretted when she raised her doe eyes up to meet his. The picture she painted sent the blood rushing to his groin.

"I'm so sorry!"

"Not a problem," he ground out, well aware he still had a grip on her shoulders. Zim held his breath for a heartbeat. Two. Three. And tried to will away his growing erection.

When she leaned back, Zim released her.

"Thanks." Her smile was a little shy and a lot sexy. "This seat taken?"

"Uh, no." Zim helped her ease the stool back, careful not to touch her again. If he did, he might not be able to stop.

He couldn't remember the last time he'd had such an immediate, physical reaction to a woman.

"New digs, eh?" Camden set four coasters down on the bar. "First round's on me, then."

"Aww, thanks, Cam! You're a gem." Jo took a seat next to the redhead. The fourth girl, who looked a lot like the brunette – sister, maybe? - sat between them.

Zim grabbed his beer and took a healthy swig. It was damned hard not to look at the gorgeous creature sitting mere inches from him. He failed, taking a long, lingering glance. And he got caught, not by the brunette but by the blonde.

She smiled, winking. "Hey."

Zim gave her a firm nod, tipping back the rest of his pint. "Hi."

"See something you like?"

Zim nearly choked on his drink. "What?"

His sputter got the raven-haired beauty's attention, and she turned to look at him.

Jo's smile turned devilish. "This is my friend-"

"Sue." The brunette interrupted. "I'm Sue."

The blonde looked confused but shrugged. "And you are?"

"Con," he answered after a beat, nearly spilling his real name.

"Hi, Con. I'm Jo, that's Lovie," she said pointing at the redhead. "And this is Amri, Sue's sister. So if you have designs on her, you'd better come correct."

Amri and Jo laughed, Lovie rolled her eyes, but Sue…Sue blushed, and it was the sweetest, cutest, sexiest thing Zim had ever seen. Then she surprised him by meeting his eyes.

"Nice to meet you," she said in a voice he wanted to hear first thing in the morning after making her scream all night.

Fuck.

He should have left, right then.

Cam chuckled. "Have fun, ladies, but take it easy on my mate, here. He's shy."

Zim was going to fucking kill him and ship his body back to Glasgow. Fucker. He gave him the dirtiest look he could manage, but Cam only laughed.

"You too, huh?" Sue turned back to him. "Well, we can be socially awkward together."

Zim could only nod, lost in her smile.

He felt awkward. And uncomfortable. And realized he hadn't had a one-on-one conversation with a woman he was truly attracted to in longer than he could remember.

He raised a hand to ask, but Camden was already there with another pint for him.

"I'll have what he's having," Sue said with a teasing grin.

He cleared his throat, which was a desert. "So, you're celebrating?"

She nodded, taking her first sip from her glass. It left a foam mustache across the curve of her upper lip.

Zim wanted to lick it off. Suck on that plump piece of flesh until she moaned for him.

Jeee-sus.

"Just moved into my new place. Literally." She ran the tip of one finger around her glass, her gaze following it, but her mind was clearly elsewhere.

"New in town?"

Sue shook her head, a tiny frown wrinkling the smooth skin of her forehead.

"No, just," she sighed and took another drink. "New start."

Zim's lust-clouded brain cleared enough to recognize that something bad had happened to this woman, and he felt all of his senses tune into her for the slightest hint of what it was. And what he could do about it. He wanted to fix it, whatever it was. Put the smile back on her face.

Sue glanced at him before looking away again. "It's the classic tale of girl meets boy, boy proposes to girl, boy turns out to be a cheating douchebag, moves out in the middle of the day, and leaves a Dear John letter.

Fuck. "Ouch."

Another glance from her and a smile so sad it made Zim irrationally angry. He wanted to find the idiot that hurt this woman and knock his dick in the dirt. Well, first he'd ask why the hell he'd walked out on someone so sweet, and then he'd knock his dick in the dirt.

"Yeah." Another sigh, another sip, and another smile for him, this one brighter. Full of hope, somehow. "Anyway, that's my story. What's yours?"

"I'm…in town for a few days. On business." Not a lie, exactly.

Something flashed across her features. Disappointment? Her shoulders seemed to deflate a tiny bit.

"Ah. Well," Sue raised her glass and waited for Zim to do the same. "I hope you have a successful visit."

"Thanks."

"Try to have some fun while you're here, Philly's a great town. Lots to see and do."

"I like what I've seen so far." It was as cheesy a line as they came, but mission accomplished.

Sue's smile returned, accompanied by another blush. She was going to kill him with those, and he'd die with a grin on his face.

"Hey, Cam!" Jo's voice brought the Scot down to their end of the bar. "Can I play DJ tonight?"

Cam grinned. "O'course, love. You know I love it when you do."

He handed her a remote. A few seconds later, a thumping dance track poured through the speakers, transforming the dark little pub into a dark little club as people started to move to the music.

Two hours later, Zim found himself on a makeshift dance floor with an armful of hot, ebony-haired, Bambi-eyed vixen.

Sue draped herself over him like a well-worn jersey, soft and way too comfortable.

Zim was done for.

He wanted her. Just a taste of her.

Right the hell now.

CHAPTER 3

JESUS CHRIST, this guy was hot. Like, *I don't care what your name is* hot. Like, *I don't even care what you do for a living because I just want to climb you like a jungle gym*, hot.

Suji didn't know what the hell the alcohol content was in the beer she'd been drinking, but she couldn't remember feeling this mellow. Or this turned on.

And this Con guy was sexy as hell. Tall and broad with chestnut hair and teasing, dark chocolate eyes. His mouth was wide with cupid's bow lips and she couldn't stop staring at them while they sat at the bar.

Now he was grinding up on her like she was a scratch pole and he was the world's neediest cat. Or maybe she was the one doing the grinding. It was, after all, *her* ass pressed against his crotch.

Con wrapped his arm around her waist, and Suji threw her arm back around his neck. His breath tickled her neck as he spoke into it.

"You're driving me fucking crazy."

"Ditto," she replied, though it came out more like "unnnngh."

It was the music, she reasoned. A thumping bass line over a tight drum pattern that made her hips move of their own volition. Damn Jo and her wicked taste in music.

Next to them, on the dance floor they'd created by pushing several tables to the side, her sister wiggled and swayed along with Jo, and Jo's friend Lovie. All three of them seemed to be having a blast. Especially Jo, who had snagged the bashful, young waiter and forced the poor kid to dance.

He wasn't suffering, by the looks of it. And Suji certainly wasn't having a bad time herself.

Her skin prickled, a combination of sweat and need as Con moved to the music with her. They were practically glued together, and there was no mistaking the effect it had on him.

Lips brushed her neck, setting her blood on fire.

"Is this okay?" He voice rumbled just beneath the sound of the bass guitar.

Suji nodded, breathless.

Con turned her in his arms, wrapping them around her waist. He trapped her leg between his thighs and pulled her in tight.

Suji looped her arms around his neck. He smelled delicious, like leather, and sweat, and man.

"Fuck," he said when she rolled her body into his. "I, fuck."

"Want to?"

Whoa, Nelly. Did she just...?

Con slowed them down, their movements lazy compared to the frenetic pulse of the music, and of her racing heart. He leaned back to meet her gaze. His was hooded and kept dropping down to her mouth.

"Say that again," he demanded, licking his lips.

"I don't normally..."

"I didn't think you did."

"But I want..."

"God, I need..."

He groaned when Suji stretched up to run her nose along the column of his neck. She wanted to bite him. Mark him. Where this was all coming from, she had no idea. Nor did she care.

She grabbed his hand and pulled him toward the back of the pub.

Jo caught her eye as they passed and gave her an enthusiastic thumbs-up.

Amrita arched an eyebrow but thankfully didn't comment. Suji didn't want to question it. She didn't want to think. She wanted to feel.

They got as far as the darkened hall that led to the bathrooms before he spun her up against the wood paneling and smashed his mouth down over hers.

The kiss was brutal, unrelenting, and exactly what Suji needed to survive the apocalypse, or so she told herself.

She had never been kissed like this. Had never been grabbed like this, like he couldn't get enough of her body in his hands. Suji shook, trembled, quaked with need and Con hadn't even touched her yet. Not where she needed to be touched.

"Con," she gasped when they came up for air.

"Tell me what you want."

"You expect me to think?" Suji laughed, a sound so carefree and light she didn't recognize the sound of it. When had she ever felt like this? When had Brian ever made her feel so wanted?

Con slowed again, threading a hand through her hair and making her dizzy. He really knew how to use those massive hands of his.

"I can take charge if that's what you want."

Suji nodded or thought she did. Her head was suddenly spinning.

"Look at me, sweetness." He tipped her chin up and waited until she met his eyes, which took a bit longer than it should have. "Hey, I don't know if this is such a good idea."

"I'm all right." She thought she said. Her tongue felt thick, and her stomach began to roil and bubble. Was it super warm in the hall?

He frowned. "I think you're the opposite of fine."

Suddenly, they were moving. Panic gripped her for a moment until she felt the cool air on her face. They were in the alley behind the bar.

"Breathe." His voice had shifted from consummation to concern. "Do you think you're going to be sick?"

"I…" Now that he had mentioned it, a wave of nausea hit her. "Shit."

Suji doubled over.

Con held her hair while she vacated the contents of her stomach, which were entirely liquid. Dinner, she'd forgotten to eat dinner. Suji had never been one of those people who could party on an empty stomach.

"Stupid."

"Nah," he argued, producing a napkin out of thin air. He gently wiped her mouth after she stood upright. "I'm betting you haven't eaten much today. You said you moved into a new place, right? Lots of lifting and carrying, I bet."

Suji nodded and regretted it immediately. "I'm so embarrassed."

"Don't be. I'm the one who's embarrassed. I should have realized…" He trailed off, still holding her hair up off her neck. His touch was more comforting than it should have been for someone she barely knew.

Suji became aware of just how alone they were, and how dark the alley was.

Seeming to sense her discomfort, Con withdrew his hand and put some distance between them.

"You ready to head back inside? I'm sure Camden can rustle up something in the kitchen for you."

"No, thanks. I'm going to grab my purse and head home. It's been a long day."

If she'd been thinking any more clearly, Suji might have trusted her eyes more because it looked like his face fell.

"Right." He shoved his hands into his pockets.

Suji hadn't realized how tall he was, at least six-foot-four, or how dark his eyes were. Almost black. But nothing was threatening about him. He was actually kinda…sweet. Sweet and sexy, what a combo.

"I could give you my number if you want to…" *Pick up where we left off?* Suji wasn't sure where that sentence was headed, but she needn't have bothered.

His gaze dropped to his feet. "Like I said, I'm leaving town in a couple of days."

"Oh." Of course, he was. "Well…"

"C'mon, let's get you back inside.

Con guided her back through the hall and into the bar, his arm strong and solid around her waist.

Amrita's head snapped up when she saw them, her eyes narrowing when she saw Suji's face.

Suji shook her head to let her know Con hadn't done anything wrong. She needed to explain as soon as they reached her, or her sister would go apeshit.

"I drank too much and ate too little."

Amri's eyes widened. "Oh no! Poor baby girl. We need to get you some food." She turned toward the bar, but Suji grabbed her arm. "Actually, I'm gonna grab a taxi and head home."

"Aww, man. Are you sure?"

"Yeah, but thanks for dragging me out. I had fun." Suji tried for a smile.

"You're in good hands, now." Con said over her shoulder. "Thanks for the dance, I'm just gonna…"

He let her go, and Suji immediately missed the contact. She watched him make his way back over to the bar.

Amri leaned in to whisper I her ear. "What about tall, dark, and fuckable?"

Suji shook her head. "Out-of-towner on his way home."

"Bummer." Amrita hugged her. "But hey, you took a big step tonight. I'm proud of you."

"Thanks, sis. I'm going to go eat something and drink a gallon of water. Work's gonna be fun tomorrow."

Amrita laughed. "Yeah, good luck with that."

Suji reckoned she'd need more than luck.

CHAPTER 4

IT WAS the smell that got to him. The deceptively antiseptic smell of sickness, fading dreams and lost hopes. That's what Zim couldn't stand. And after last night, he could barely tolerate the stench. No more Belhaven for him.

Ever.

Zim took a deep breath and tried to acclimate himself as quickly as possible. He didn't know how anyone could work in a hospital, day in and day out. As a professional hockey player, he was used to pain. Used to blood, and sweat, and the stench of exertion. This was different. Nausea threatened to swallow him.

"Thanks for coming by, Mr. Zimin. Could I get you anything?" Dr. Calvin Morris, head of Pediatrics at The Hospital of the University of Philadelphia, sat across from Zim, offering him a friendly smile.

Zim returned it. "No, thanks. And call me Zim."

The doctor's smile brightened. "Zim it is. I'm Calvin."

"Nice to put a face to the name."

"Likewise."

Calvin folded his hands and rested them on his surprisingly uncluttered desk. The entire office was spartan, but was flooded with natural light from the enormous window behind his office chair. It offered an unobstructed view of the Philadelphia skyline.

"Again, let me say how wonderful it is that you want to make our department the beneficiary of your foundation. The way things are going, donations and grants are getting harder to come by."

"Yeah, I'm aware. And I hope I can help."

"I know you can," Calvin reassured him. "You already have, just by making us a stop on your Cup Day tour. Congratulations again on the win. I bet it was thrilling, being on an expansion team and winning the big one practically right out of the gate."

"Thank you and, yes, it was pretty gratifying. But this isn't really a tour. I'm just going to drop by my parents, stop by here, and then we have the fundraiser tomorrow night."

"Really?" Calvin cocked his head. "Nothing fun, like, drinking champagne out of it? I hear that's a thing."

Zim shrugged, smiling. "Maybe I'll get together with some friends from the neighborhood."

"Where did you grow up?"

"Mayfair."

"Ah, I didn't know that. You were born in Russia, weren't you?"

Zim nodded. "Yeah, in St. Petersburg, but I was twelve when my family emigrated."

"I see. And your…" Calvin paused, caution in his eyes. "Your sister was diagnosed in Russia?"

The mention of his sister brought forth a familiar ache, but Zim pushed it aside. Ten years had done nothing to diminish the impact of his loss.

"Yeah. Mila was diagnosed there, but the facilities to treat her weren't great."

"Your family learned of Dr. Kohn's program here at THUP?"

"We were fortunate." Zim had to swallow the lump in his throat before he could continue. "My father had enough money to bring us here. And we had family here already, so it was easier for us than for most others to immigrate."

"Very fortunate, indeed."

"Yes."

"I'm sorry for asking, but, the treatment…?"

"It was successful, to a point. We got seven more years with Mila."

"You were very close?"

"Twins."

The other man nodded, his lips thinning into a sad smile. "Well, we are honored that you want to establish your sister's trust here at THUP."

Calvin turned to his computer monitor. "I see here that all of the paperwork has been filed. Your lawyer is very thorough."

"You have no idea."

"Meticulous, is he?"

"Yes, she is. My hope is to expand the program someday, have something like this available in different cities."

Morris nodded, smiling. "Well, I see no reason why the board wouldn't approve it."

"Good. By the way, that dinner tomorrow night is sold out, but I have seats reserved for you and the members of the board if you want to bring your spouse."

"Whereabouts?"

"The Manayunk."

"Oh, that's a fantastic restaurant. Thanks for the invitation, I'll ask my wife." Calvin knit his fingers behind his head. "I remember when the Manayunk was first docked at Penn's Landing. They gave tours of the old ship, you know. It was like stepping back in time."

"I bet. Since the weather's been holding up, I thought it would be a good spot to wine and dine the deep pockets. People can get professional photos with The Cup."

Calvin hummed in agreement. "Will the press be there?"

"I don't really do press."

"I've heard that about you," the other man teased. "Not often you come across a professional athlete, much less one that's just won the biggest prize in his sport, who isn't ready to shout it from the rooftops and appear on every TV show that'll have him."

Zim shook his head. "It's never been my style."

"I see. But you're alright with the small contingent we have scheduled to come in tomorrow?"

"Tomorrow? You invited the press?"

"Yes, but only the newspapers. I know you didn't want any television coverage. And I've already informed security, and the staff, should anyone try to crash the event. Parents and visitors already have to sign in."

"Thanks, I appreciate it."

"It isn't just for you, it's about the children. They are as yet unaware. We want it to be a surprise for them, you understand."

"It'll be fun, I hope. I've hired a balloon guy, and a woman who does magic for kids."

"Sounds great. I must warn you, though," Calvin leaned forward as if about to share a terrible secret. "My Head Nurse, Sujarta Meriwether, she's...well, she's not too excited to have you here."

"Oh?"

"She is dedicated, one of the best nurses I've ever worked with, and she is fabulous with the kids. They all fall in love with her, and she's very protective."

"My sister had a nurse like that, awesome lady."

"The staff at THUP is exceptional, always has been." The man's pride was evident.

"That's why I chose you." Zim stood. "Anyway, I should probably get out of your hair."

Calvin rose from his chair, his hand extended. "I'll see you tomorrow. If there's anything you need, don't hesitate to call my assistant. By the way, would it be an imposition if I brought my Buffalo 'Subzero' jersey in for you to sign?"

"You're a fan?"

The older man beamed, his smile knocking ten years off his age. "Who isn't? You may keep away from the cameras, but everyone knows your reputation on the ice."

Zim smiled. "Thanks, and of course I'll sign it."

"Great! Let me see you out."

Calvin stepped around his desk and walked to the door, opening it.

Zim moved to walk through and suddenly found himself with an armful of soft, fragrant curves.

His heart stopped.

Sue, dressed in purple scrubs with a cartoon turtle print, blinked up at him. Apparently, she'd been about to knock on the door before she landed in his arms.

He liked having here there again.

Zim had only a moment to take in her high cheekbones, wide almond eyes, and flawless henna skin before she recovered from the shock and stepped back to address the man she'd come to see, ignoring him completely. Like they were strangers. Like she'd never seen him before.

Just how drunk had she been?

"Dr. Morris, tell me you're not really going let that guy come in here tomorrow for a photo op? Things are hectic enough without some meathead jock bringing a flippin' media circus into the ward."

Jock? It wasn't untrue. He was a professional athlete, after all. But meathead? Zim stood to the side and watched the exchange with amusement.

Calvin exhaled slowly, giving him a quick look of apology before addressing her.

"Nurse Meriwether, I promise you it won't be a media circus."

"How could it not be?" Her tone was one of exasperation. "He's bringing some big trophy, or whatever, and who knows what else. Team mascot or something?"

"He plays for New Orleans, Ms. Meriwether. I don't think we'd do well to have another team's colors in The Hospital of the University of Philadelphia."

"Then why is he coming? Tell him to stay down there. He can throw a parade on Bourbon Street."

Zim chuckled. He liked this woman. "Because I'm from here. And I wanted to bring The Cup to Philly, even if it isn't with the hometown team at the moment."

Her eyes flashed with surprise when she turned to him. "You're…"

He grinned. "The meathead jock."

He expected her to flush with embarrassment, perhaps make an apology for speaking so harshly. Maybe even acknowledge that they'd had their tongues down each other's throats not ten hours ago. What he didn't expect was for her to aim her frustrations directly at him.

"Look, no offense, I don't care where you're from or where you play, I just don't want a circus around my ward."

"I don't intend…"

"And, really, I'm sure you have better things to do that pretend to care about a bunch of sick kids."

"Suji," Calvin warned.

Not-Sue-but-Suji sighed with undisguised disgust. "I know, I know. Sorry, but these children come first."

"For all of us, Ms. Meriwether." There was no ire in his voice. Calvin clearly admired this woman and Zim could see why.

She was beautiful, yes. He already knew that. But there was something about her spirit, about the way she'd so clearly taken to heart her commitment to her work that Zim liked. A lot.

She'd shown the same genuine sweetness and concern for him last night.

He wanted to know more about her, more than what she looked like naked, which was odd. He never wanted to get to know anyone, really. Other than his parents, he stuck with his friends and his teammates, most of which fell into the same net.

"I'm told the only press will be newspaper." Zim looked to Calvin for confirmation, and the other man nodded.

Suji eyed him with suspicion. "No T.V.?"

"Mr. Zimin insisted that no TV cameras be present," the doctor supplied.

"Then…why?" Her eyes narrowed as she sized Zim up.

"Mr. Zimin is launching a foundation to help children with long-term illnesses and their families."

The brunette arched an eyebrow. Her eyes were a rusty gold, like amber, and just as hard. "Of course he is."

It wasn't exactly disdain Zim heard in her voice, but it was damn close. He wondered what in her past had left her with such an intense dislike of pro athletes. Sure, a lot of them had reputations, but most of the guys he worked with were decent people. Or maybe it was just him.

He scoured his memory for anything he might have done last night to upset her. Maybe he had pushed too hard? Kissed her too soon? Too much? Not enough?

"We can discuss it later," Calvin promised her before turning to Zim. "I'm sorry, I have an appointment across campus, but I'll see you tomorrow. You can find your way from here?"

Zim watched with amusement as Suji's expression flashed from surprise, to defeat, to annoyance.

"Maybe Nurse Meriwether could be my guide."

The look she gave him was murderous. What had he done to her last night? As far as he remembered, he'd been a perfect gentleman.

Though, now, he was staring. He couldn't help it.

Suji's eyes widened slightly before a frown settled over them.

"I'll leave you to it." Calvin grinned before stepping around them and breaking into a light jog.

Suji pointed to their right. "The elevator's over there. She spun on her rubber-clogged heel and walked away.

Despite being totally out of his element, Zim found himself following her as she briskly moved through the ward, breezing by the nurse's station to grab a clipboard. They ended up in a room that housed four beds, and Suji went to one by the windows. The outline of a small, thin frame could be seen under the hospital blanket. The sight of it stopped Zim mid-stride. He stood and watched as she closed the curtain around the bed, not even sparing him a glance.

Well, damn.

"Do you belong here?"

The little girl had nearly given him a heart attack, her voice sounded so much like his sister's. Like Mila's, at that age.

Zim swallowed hard and then turned to find the source of the inquiry staring up at him with big, pale green eyes. The bruising underneath them told him the child was suffering, even if her pale pink pajamas and hospital gown hadn't given her away. The closely-cropped, ginger hair that swept over her too-visible scalp made another lump form in Zim's throat.

"Hi."

"Hi." She blinked up at him, her face a perfect mask of impatience. "You didn't answer my question."

"Do I belong here?"

"Did I stutter?"

Ten, maybe eleven years old, and already a cynic. Zim smiled.

"No, you didn't. I'm sorry. I was visiting with Dr. Morris, but he had to go to a meeting."

"Oh." Her face relaxed from suspicion to curiosity. "What are you going to do now?"

Her question surprised him. Zim had a few hours before he had to go to the airport to collect Edwin Motz, the official Keeper of the Hockey League's prized trophy, The Cup.

For the next twenty-four hours, plus a few extra, thanks to scheduling, The Cup would be his to do with as he pleased. Within reason.

"I'm not sure, actually. Any suggestions?"

To his surprise, the young girl took his hand and started walking. He had no choice but to follow. One of the other nurses looked up as they passed her station, her eyebrow raised.

"I'm taking him to the game room," the girl said without stopping.

"What did I tell you about pestering strangers, young lady?"

Zim tried to halt their progress, ready to explain to the new nurse that he meant no harm when the girl stopped and spun around to face her.

"He's not a stranger, he's Constantine Zimin, also known as Subzero, star defenseman for the New Orleans Cajun Rage, the winners of this year's League Cup. He played in eighty-four games, scored thirteen goals, had thirty-two assists, and served ninety-eight minutes in the Sin Bin."

"The Sin Bin?" The nurse, now clearly amused, folded her arms. Apparently, this sort of thing wasn't unusual for her. For Zim it was mind-blowing.

This little girl knew his stats better than he did.

The little redhead rolled her eyes. "Duh. That's the penalty box. Really, Nurse Jordan, you need to watch a game with me."

Nurse Jordan chuckled, her smooth, copper skin crinkling with her laughter. "I guess I should. Is that why you're dragging this nice, young man to the game room?"

"I want him to meet Aaron. He's a big fan."

Nurse Jordan trained her all-too-knowing eyes on Zim, and he straightened.

"I should probably get going."

"If Red, here, wants you to do something, you'd better do it Mr. Sports Star," she laughed and Zim grinned.

"Yes, ma'am." He turned back to the little girl, who had grabbed his hand again. "Lead the way."

***

The game room was a pretty cheery, given the location. They'd situated it in the corner of the building, and the room was flooded with lots of natural sunlight. Pint-sized furniture had been placed around the floor space, and low shelves lined the walls, stuffed with games and toys of every shape and size. A sectional sat in one corner, facing an entertainment center with various video game consoles.

On the sofa sat a small boy, his face screwed up in concentration as he stared at the flat screen television. He gripped the controller in his hands like a lifeline, twisting it this way and that to control the figure on the screen.

Which happened to be Zim.

"See?" Little Red pulled him along, toward the sofa.

"Aaron," her voice changed. She spoke to him as someone might talk to a skittish cat. "Hey, buddy, look."

The boy didn't respond.

Tiff dropped Zim's hand and moved toward Aaron. It was only when she stood next to him that Zim noticed the IV pole. A bag of clear liquid hung from one of the loops, and a tube extended down toward the child's arm.

Zim shoved his hands into his pockets. "Hey, little guy."

The boy glanced over his shoulder and his eyes grew wide. The controller slipped from his fingers as he stared.

33

"Don't freak out," came Tiff's warning.

"You're…"

"Hi." Zim walked around to face him, squatting low to meet him at eye level. "I'm Zim, and you're Aaron?"

"But…how…" He stuttered, his voice weak. "Are you my wish?"

Zim frowned and glanced at Tiff. "Wish?"

"He means, are you here because of the Wish Foundation. He wrote a letter asking to meet you." Tiff cocked her head. "Is that why you're here?"

"Well, no. I didn't know about it, but I'm glad to meet you, Aaron."

Aaron's smile spread slowly. A bit of red dotted his olive cheeks. "I'm Aaron."

Zim chuckled.

"He knows that, idiot," Tiff chided. "He just called you by name."

"Oh." Aaron's wide eyes followed Zim as he stood.

"If you're not his wish, what are you doing here?" Tiff was very direct, he had to give her that.

Zim checked around for other people before turning back to them. He lowered his voice to a whisper as if he were about to share a secret.

"I'll tell you, but you can't say anything to anyone."

Tiffany took a step back, frowning. "We're not supposed to keep secrets."

Zim smiled. "This one is okay, I think. I'm coming back here tomorrow, and I'm bringing The Cup with me."

"No way!" Aaron's voice grew a little stronger, but it looked like it took a lot out of him. "Here? Really? That is my wish!"

Tiff's smile was full of affection as she watched the younger boy's reaction, but she eyed Zim with suspicion.

"Are you really?"

"Yep."

Tiff nodded once. "That's pretty cool. We can keep that secret."

"Whew, thanks." Zim wiped his forehead with the back of his hand. "I'd be in big trouble if everyone found out."

"We won't tell," Aaron blurted out. "Promise."

"We pinky swear," Tiff agreed, extending hers to Zim.

Zim wrapped his pinky around hers, and they shook. He repeated the gesture with Aaron, careful not to jostle him too much.

"Thanks, guys. I appreciate it. And I might bring something extra special for you tomorrow, for being such good sports."

"A jersey!" Aaron was practically vibrating, he was so excited.

Zim chuckled. "We'll see, little man. I should get going for now."

Aaron's face fell.

"Don't worry, I'll be back tomorrow."

"You promise?"

Zim nodded. "I promise."

Unless Sujarta Meriwether had her way.

Zim decided to get going while the going was good. He turned and had made it as far as the door when he felt a tug on his shirt.

"Hey, Subzero?"

"What's up, Tiff?"

"You're really coming back tomorrow, right?" She placed her little hands on her little hips, challenging him.

"I promised I would."

Tiff's eyes narrowed as she studied him. Her judgmental gaze actually made him squirm.

"Don't break your promise, Aaron would get really upset. And then I'd get mad. And you don't want me mad. I'll go on every hockey forum and tell them how shitty you were."

"Whoa!" Zim leaned back. "Language."

Tiff shrugged. "I just wanted to be clear."

"How old are you?"

"Old enough to know a liar when I see one."

Ouch.

"See you tomorrow, Tiff."

"I better," came Tiff's reply as the elevator doors closed.

CHAPTER 5

SUJI FINISHED CHECKING the vitals on her newest patient, a seven-year-old who had gotten hit by his neighbor's car while riding his bike. Little Maurice would be okay, thank goodness. Just a few cuts and bruises. They'd kept him overnight for observation, just in case. But Suji was glad to be able to tell his parents that he would be okay.

A bit of good news in an already crazy day. Tomorrow wasn't shaping up to be any better.

Con was the jock? Of course, Con was the jock, that's just how the universe rolled when it came to Sujarta Meriwether.

Hey, Suji, sweetie, baby, we know you don't put yourself out there often, so here's the hottest man you've ever seen. But wait, you're gonna hurl on his shoes and run home like a coward. And then we'll send him to your workplace to cause all kinds of hell for you. Sound fun?

No. It didn't sound like fun at all.

Hot, hunky man aside, there was enough chaos around the ward without throwing a photo-opportunistic football player, or whatever he was, into the mix. Nevermind that Con was built like the Great Wall and looked like some ancient, Greek statue, with his chiseled jawline and full, wide mouth. Suji didn't need him or his media circus disturbing the children. Or her.

She rounded the corner just in time to catch sight the man himself as he stepped into the elevator. Suji ducked behind a file cabinet before he could see her. Of course, it had nothing to do with wanting to get another peek at him before the doors closed.

"Friend of yours?"

Mimi Jordan, one of the ward's acute care nurse practitioners, snuck up on Suji, scaring her half to death in the process.

"No." Suji stepped out of her hiding place. It wasn't a lie, exactly. They weren't friends just because they'd spent the better part of last night getting sweaty on a dance floor.

"He's the guy coming here tomorrow for a photo op with the director. Apparently, he won some sports trophy and needs to balance out his undoubtedly obscene paycheck by pretending to give a shit about sick kids."

"Wow." Mimi crossed her arms and studied Suji. "Project much?"

"What do you mean?" Suji walked over to the nurses' station. They had several patients scheduled for release, including young Maurice, and she wanted to make sure their paperwork was in order.

Mimi followed close behind.

"It couldn't be that you're lumping that guy in with your ex, could it?"

"What? No. I-I only just met Con…er…the guy, and didn't even really do that." Suji was a horrible liar. She could feel her cheeks burning and turned away to cover. "He was in Dr. Morris's office when I went to talk to him about canceling the whole thing. I just find it reprehensible that anyone would use a place like this to make themselves look good in the press, especially someone who gets paid to bash others' heads in for a living."

"He's a boxer?"

"Er…no. Football."

"Ah."

Suji paused. "I think, anyway it doesn't matter. I don't like it, and I don't want him here."

"I don't know, Suji," Mimi hedged. "He didn't seem so bad."

"You spoke to him?"

"Briefly. Tiffany accosted him before he left."

"She what?"

Tiffany Bradford was one of Suji's very first patients. Six years ago, she had been diagnosed with acute lymphoblastic leukemia. Suji had been her nurse before the young girl had been put on an experimental treatment that allowed her to return home. A treatment that had proven very successful. Tiffany was four at the time.

Typically a chatty, precocious child, it had broken Suji's heart to see her back in Dr. Morris's office two months ago. Tiffany had sat quietly in the chair, listening to Calvin explain to her parents that her cancer had indeed returned.

"What did she do? What did he say?"

Mimi grinned. "She grabbed his hand and hauled him off to the game room for a while. Apparently, she knew who he was."

"Did she?"

"Yeah, she seemed really excited to meet him. Started rattling off stats at me when I didn't recognize the guy." Mimi chuckled, shaking her head.

"Stats?"

"Something about goal percentages, I don't know." She shrugged. "I watch figure skating and tennis. The rest is lost on me."

Suji looked toward the game room, hoping for a glimpse of the little imp. "I'll have to have a chat with Tiff about talking to strangers."

"We kept an eye on them," Mimi assured her.

"Oh, I know." Suji gave her a reassuring smile. "But, still."

Mim grabbed a notepad and a pen. "So, what do we need to do to prepare for tomorrow?"

"Who's on the roster?"

Mimi stepped around the desk and sat in one of the chairs in front of a monitor. "According to the schedule, Patsy…"

"Oh good." Suji exhaled. "She'll keep things from getting out of hand."

"Yeah, no kidding. Tim will be here until eleven, and it looks like the twins are on the overlapping shift. I'll be in too. Plus the nursing students."

The twins weren't actually related but were so similar in appearance and temperament that the nickname had stuck. Suji had an excellent staff. The best, in her opinion. As the youngest Head Nurse in the hospital's history, Suji didn't need any fuck-ups on her watch. She ran her ward like a ship. The nursing students could be a handful, but they weren't her problem.

"Between our group and the students, we should be able to handle the shitshow this is bound to be."

Mimi raised one perfectly manicured eyebrow. "Wow, you really aren't expecting much, are you?"

"Dr. Morris mentioned something about him donating money to the new ward or something. That's the only reason I'm not putting a stop to the whole thing altogether."

Mimi sighed dreamily. "But he seemed so nice, and he is exceedingly easy on the eyes."

Suji shrugged, finding a sudden interest in a stack of clipboards on the counter. "I guess."

"You guess?"

"I didn't really look."

"Oh my God, you are such a fibber. Of course, you looked," Mimi teased, giving her a playful shove.

Suji laughed. Mimi had no idea.

"Who pissed in your cornflakes this morning?"

"No one, I just hate opportunists."

"Okay, I get that, but you're making a whole lot of snap judgments about a guy you only spoke to for thirty seconds."

Mimi had a point. They'd spent a whole hell of a lot more than thirty seconds together, but Suji wasn't about to admit it. "Whatever, he'll have every opportunity to prove me wrong, but I'm not expecting much."

"Harsh."

"I know. Hey, could you double check Maurice Hudson's discharge papers? His parents should be here soon to pick him up."

"Sure thing." Mimi grabbed a notepad and a pen and began scribbling.

"Thanks."

"Hi Suji!"

She turned to find Tiffany walking toward her. "Well, hello there, young lady. I heard you had quite an eventful morning."

"I did! Subzero was here, and I took him to meet Aaron because he's, like, a huge fan." The little girl practically bounced in her slippered feet. Her eyes seemed a little brighter today, and there was honest-to-goodness color in her cheeks.

Suji smiled, all thoughts of chastisement chased away by Tiffany's obvious excitement.

"Oh yeah? Are you a fan too?"

Tiffany nodded, toying with the drawstring on her robe. "Yeah, of course. He's the best defenseman in the league. At least I think so."

"What league is that?"

Tiffany glared at Suji as if she'd asked her the color of the sun. "Uh, the hockey league."

"He's a hockey player?"

"Duh," Tiffany groaned. "Cup-winning Cajun Rage? Desjardins Trophy winner for Best Defenseman?"

Suji could only stare blankly. She glanced at Mimi who grinned wide but kept her eyes trained on the monitor. The least she could do was step in with some Google facts or something.

"Sounds...impressive."

Tiffany's eye roll was epic. "I swear, nurse Suji, you people have a lot to learn about sports. But don't worry, I can teach you."

"Great, you can do that later." Suji reached down to fix the collar of Tiffany's robe, which had slipped, exposing the bandage that covered a new lesion. "How were we with breakfast this morning?"

Tiffany scrunched up her nose. "Okay."

Suji narrowed her eyes. "Define okay."

"I ate the applesauce."

"That's good, honey, but we need some protein too, remember? We had a talk about that."

"I know," Tiffany whined. "But everything tastes like butt."

Mimi barked out a laugh.

Suji stifled one too. "Tiff, I know things don't taste very good for you right now. It's the side-effect..."

"Of my medicine, I know, but I can't, like, force it down my throat."

"Okay, how about you eat one boiled egg for me, and I'll get you one of those chocolate shakes."

In actuality, they were meal replacement smoothies, but Tiffany didn't need to know that.

The little girl's face lit up like the fourth of July. "Really?"

"Sure, sweetie."

"Could I have salt on the egg? It helps with the taste."

"I'll get you a little salt. Now head on back to your room, and I'll bring you a tray. Okay?"

Tiffany offered her a salute. "Yes, ma'am."

Behind her, Mimi chuckled. "That child is something else."

"That she is."

"And your hockey boyfriend is too, take a look."

Suji rounded the desk to stand behind Mimi, who had indeed been busy on Google. She's pulled up several photos of Subzero, a/k/a Constantine Zimin, and…wow. The images didn't do him justice, though. Having been up close and personal with the man, Suji knew the real thing was so much prettier. And tastier. And solid like granite.

And she needed to pull the emergency brake on that train of thought.

"I wouldn't mind going a few rounds with him. Damn," Mimi drawled.

"Rounds?"

"Uh, quarters? I know nothing about hockey."

"That makes two of us," Suji admitted. "What's this trophy he's supposedly bringing?"

"Says here he plays for the New Orleans Cajun Rage and that they won the hockey championship this year. I guess that's the trophy he's bringing here tomorrow."

Mimi pointed to a photo of a player hoisting a large, silver chalice over his head in celebration.

"Oh and he's from here, apparently," Mimi supplied as she scrolled through an ESPN article. "It's weird, though."

"What is?" Suji busied herself with paperwork, not at all interesting in knowing more about Constantine Zimin.

"There's not a whole lot information about this guy."

"What do you mean?"

"Well, when I search for him, the only stuff that comes up is hockey stats and a bit about him as a player." Mimi continued to scroll, and Suji continued to not peer over her shoulder. "Nothing personal. No photos of him out and about. No women, no family, nothing. It's like he doesn't exist outside of his sport."

"He probably has a publicist to keep his nose clean."

"Or," Mimi countered. "He's just very private."

"Maybe," Suji conceded. "Whatever the case, he'd better behave himself tomorrow, or I'll kick his ass out of here and toss that trophy right out into the street."

Mimi saluted, mimicking Tiffany. "Yes, ma'am."

Suji laughed. "Don't you start."

"You have to admit," Mimi said, flipping through image after image of Constantine Zimin. "He's damn sexy."

"I don't have to admit that at all.".

She didn't. Not out loud, anyway.

CHAPTER 6

ZIM PULLED into Philadelphia International Airport with twenty minutes to spare. He found a space in short-term parking and decided to give Jonas a call.

"Hey knucklehead."

"Zim! What's up, asshole? I just got off the phone with Thibs," Jonas spoke in his soft, Swedish accent that the puck bunnies seemed to love.

"Yeah? How is the old man?"

"Strong enough to kick your ass if he ever heard you call him old," Jonas replied, laughing.

Until very recently, Jonas "Iceman" Magnussen was a center for the New Orleans Cajun Rage. In the rink, he and Zim had made quite a pair. The press had nicknamed them Fire and Ice because Zim's temper had often gotten the better of him before he learned to channel his frustrations into his skating and puck handling. Meanwhile, Jonas had always been known as the calm one, until he became more aggressive on the ice, racking up more penalty minutes than a center should.

"Good to hear it. How are things with you? Glad to be back home?"

"It's strange to be back, but really good too," Jonas replied. From the tone of his voice, Zim could tell how pleased he really was and he knew why.

"And how is Mariam?"

"She's great. We're…we're doing great."

"That's awesome, man."

When Jonas started out in the league, he'd made the choice to leave both Sweden and his girlfriend behind. Though, to hear Jonas talk about it, Mariam had pretty much made the choice for him. Still, it was good to hear the guy sound so happy and settled.

Magnussen was a magician with a stick in his hands, and Zim was the guy who always had his back. Until the one time he didn't.

In game six of The Cup finals, Zim had given the Spartans a chance at a power play by taking a stupid penalty against Alec Crenshaw. Zim could only sit in the Sin Bin and watch in horror as Crenshaw plowed into Jonas and sent him sprawling awkwardly into the boards.

Time had stopped while the medical team tended to him on the ice, treating him so gingerly Zim wasn't sure if he was even still alive. The replay on the Jumbotron confirmed just how horrific the crash had been, displaying Jonas's leg bent at an unnatural angle. There had been a collective gasp from the crowd. Zim's heart had been in his throat for the entire seven minutes and six seconds that Jonas lay there, still as death.

He'd never forgive himself for leaving him vulnerable.

Yes, there were other defensemen on their team. Good guys. Talented guys. But Jonas was Zim's responsibility, and he'd let him down. Had let the team down. Only the fact that Zim had protected their lead in game seven, helping out their goalie with a kick save in the waning seconds, had eased his conscience a bit. Jonas didn't blame him, of course. That's just the kind of guy he was.

"By the way, I'm back on the ice."

Zim smiled. "Really?"

"Yeah, just coaching some local kids. I may even start up my own camp."

Pride filled the man's voice, and Zim was relived to hear it. He had a lingering fear that Jonas had left the game with reservations.

"Seems like being a Cup winner carries quite a bit of prestige."

Zim chuckled. "You don't say. No second-thoughts about staying over there?"

"Zero."

Even though Jonas couldn't see him, Zim nodded. "I'm happy for you, dude."

"Thanks. So, when are you going to settle down with someone?"

"Honestly, it's not even on my RADAR." Zim ignored the image of Suji Meriwether that popped into his head.

"When has it ever been?" Jonas countered. "The last semi-serious relationship I remember you having was when we were in Buffalo."

Lea. Zim shuddered. "Don't remind me."

"She wasn't the right one, but that doesn't mean anything," Jonas said, sounding very much like a life coach. "You'll never know unless you actually put yourself out there."

"Sorry, how hard did you hit your head? Are you running a matchmaking service?"

"Fuck off."

"That's more like it." Zim laughed. "Look, I'm at the airport. Motz's plane just landed."

Jonas groaned long and loud. "Good luck with that."

"Is he that bad?"

"No, I suppose he's only doing his job, but he's so regimented about your schedule. Don't let him get to you. It's your day with The Cup."

"Thanks for the tip."

"Anytime. Come for a visit soon.

"I will."

"Catch you later."

***

Edwin Motz was a wiry, wisp of a man and not at all what Zim had expected. When he emerged from baggage claim, flanked by two bodyguards, Zim thought maybe he was some tech billionaire. It wasn't until he noticed The Cup's travel container on the cart behind them that Zim knew he was the Keeper.

Motz, of course, knew exactly who Zim was.

"Thanks or being on time, Mr. Zimin." The Keeper's handshake was firm.

"Of course." Zim eyed the security detail, extending his hand to the first. "Zim."

"Tony," came the man's bassy response.

He was a six-foot-two-ish, mahogany-skinned, Black man with a shaved head and a friendly face. The gold hoops that adorned each earlobe, and the white t-shirt that stretched across his broad chest, reminded Zim of Mr. Clean.

Tony smiled back, gesturing to the guy on the other side. "This here's Jeff."

"Hey, Jeff." Zim shook the other man's hand, noting the crushing grip with amusement.

Jeff apparently wanted to make an impression. He was slightly shorter than Tony, and though they both towered over Motz, they were still shorter than Zim himself.

Jeff ran a hand through his short, blond hair. "Nice to meet you. We're with Liberty Security and we're assigned to Mr. Motz and The Cup while they're here in Philadelphia."

"So, what's your first stop, Mr. Zimin?" Motz grabbed the handle of his suitcase and the four of them started off.

Unlike most of the other players on his team, Zim hadn't been given a set schedule of appearances.

"My parents."

Motz smiled. "Of course."

After securing The Cup in the back of his black Cadillac Escalade, the four men piled into the SUV and Zim got them on their way.

"I didn't know you were from Philly," Tony said.

"Yep, my family moved here when I was a kid."

"Where'd you go to high school?" The question came from Jeff.

"St. Joe's."

"And you still live here? How come nobody knows you live here?"

Zim caught Tony's eye in the rearview mirror. "I prefer it that way."

Tony nodded, smiling. "Got it."

"Any particular events I should know about, Mr Zimin?"

"Please, call me Zim. My dad is Mr. Zimin."

"Fine then, Zim. You can call me Eddie. The rest of your team does, anyway."

"Not a fan?" Zim risked a glance over at the unassuming man.

Motz shrugged. "I've been called worse."

"Eddie it is. We have about a twenty minute drive. There's water back there, if anyone needs it. And I think I have some protein bars in the middle console."

There was rustling behind him as Jeff distributed the items.

"Thanks, man."

"No problem."

The trip took a little longer than planned, thanks to some construction on Lincoln Drive, but Zim was able to park right in front of his parents two-story, craftsman in Chestnut Hill. It was situated at the end of a tree-lined street, right at the edge of the Philadelphia city limits.

"Here we are."

"Very nice," Eddie commented.

"You get it for them?" Tony asked as they stepped out of the car.

Zim nodded. The house, though still modest, was the only big-ticket item his parents would allow him to gift them. Before he could say another word, the front door opened and Lilya Zimin burst through with a big smile and wide open arms.

"Kolya!"

"Mama." Zim bent his knees and opened his arms to his mother, squeezing her tight. "How are you?"

At five-feet and a few inches, she only came up to the center of his chest, but her personality was larger than life. She squeezed his face between her soft hands. Her smile lit up her forest green eyes.

"Let me look at you."

"Mom." Zim laughed, squirming. "You act like you haven't seen me in years. It's only been a week."

"It's a week too long. And who are your friends?" She smoothed her salt and pepper curls back from her forehead and turned to greet the other men, who all took turns shaking her hand and introducing themselves.

"Such big strong men, the two of you," she said to Tony and Jeff. "Do you perform with my son?"

"No, ma'am," Tony replied. Zim admired the tone of respect in his voice. "We're just here to keep an eye on the trophy."

"Ah, yes! "She turned back to Zim. "Your father has been on and on about the chalice."

"Cup," Eddie corrected her.

She turned to look at him, sizing him up. "You do not perform hockey."

Eddie coughed. "Er, no, Mrs. Zimin. I merely look after The Cup during its travels."

Her brow quirked. "*Shto?*"

"It's a very valuable piece of history," Jeff supplied. "And Mr. Motz, here, is in charge of its safety. Tony and I are here to assist him while he's here in Philly."

She nodded. "Ah, I see." Turning back to Eddie, she smiled. "That is a very important job, and I am sure your mother is proud of you."

Eddie actually blushed. "Er, thank you. I like to hope so. Ma'am."

"Lilechcka, why are you keeping everyone outside?" Gennady Zimin stepped out onto the landing, his voice booming with mirth. "Come inside, gentlemen. Zim, bring them in. We have food prepared."

"We?" Zim's mother stepped around him before grabbing his hand and pulling him along. That seemed to be happening a lot today.

"I helped," argued Zim's father, scratching at his graying temples.

"Yes, Genya, you started the oven for me," she deadpanned. "Thank you."

The group moved into the house, which smelled like heaven. Zim's mother was an incredible cook. And she'd apparently gone all out for the occasion. The dining room table displayed dish after dish of Russian delicacies, as well as a few American items that Zim had always loved. Namely, potato salad, macaroni and cheese, and cornbread.

"Wow," Jeff muttered. "I wasn't hungry until I walked in here."

"Well, you must eat. I made more than enough." Zim's mother pulled Jeff toward a stack of dishes. "Help yourself, we're not shy here."

"At least let him wash his hands, Lilya."

She blushed, clutching her hands to her chest. "Oh, what was I thinking? I'm just so excited to have my Kolya here for dinner."

Tony and Jeff helped Eddie remove The Cup from its case, and they set it on the sidebar at the end of the dining room.

Zim'd father slipped his glasses on and approached it as if he were visiting a shrine. While his mother fussed in the kitchen, and the other men washed up for dinner, Zim and his father shared a quiet moment with the trophy.

"I'm very proud of you, *solnyshko*."

"Thank you, papa."

"When you put on your first pair of skates, I knew." He turned to Zim, who was surprised to find his eyes shining. "I knew you would do great things. You were always so disciplined, so…focused. Both you and Mila, such beautiful skaters."

"Thanks to you, papa. If it weren't for you dragging us out onto the ice before I could barely walk, I would have never known how much I'd love it."

His father nodded and bent down and located Zim's name where it had been etched into The Cup's gleaming silver.

"This is beyond any of my expectations. To see our family name on such a thing, it's…"

He stood, covering his mouth with his fist. Zim allowed him a few moments to collect himself. His father was not an overly emotional man. To see him choked up with pride had his own eyes stinging with unshed tears.

Gennady turned and clasped Zim's shoulders. "I'm proud of you, Kolya. And your mother is proud of you, Mila would be too. So proud."

"*Spasibo*, papa."

"We all wanted this for you, this success. And we want you to be happy too. To maybe have a family of your own, someday, so you can pass your gifts along to a son. Or a daughter," he added, chuckling. He pointed at The Cup. "This is wonderful. But you need to start thinking about more than the ice, *da*?"

Zim nodded, if only to let his father know he understood. Unfortunately, he had zero prospects on the relationship front, which was his own damn fault. For some reason, his thoughts traveled back again to Suji Meriwether and her succulent mouth. And her disapproving glare.

Women like that, women who didn't care who you played for or how much money you had, they were rarely in his orbit. He'd see her again tomorrow. Maybe he'd ask her out on a proper date, ask her to accompany him to the fundraiser. What harm could it do?

Okay, it was probably a colossally stupid idea but he couldn't entirely dismiss it. There was something about her...aside from her sweet, round ass.

"Come, *angel moy*, let's eat something." Zim's mother called from the other end of the room and everyone took seats at the table.

"Mama, how many people were you expecting?"

She shrugged. "You and your father, me, and Mr. Motz."

Jesus. There was enough food on the table to feed them all for a week or more.

Zim's father leaned over and whispered into his ear.

"Whoever you find, make sure she can count properly or else your waistline will suffer." He laughed under his breath.

"Dad," Zim started around a mouthful of *piroshky*. "I wouldn't exactly call this suffering."

CHAPTER 7

SUJI HAD SLEPT like the dead. So, when her alarm went off at six-thirty in the morning, she didn't have her usual urge to hurl it across the room

Jasmine merely changed positions on her little cat bed by the dresser and went back to snoozing.

Suji's dreams had been interesting. And, much to her dismay, had featured a very tall, very broad-shouldered hockey player with amazing lips and talented hands. Of course, it had nothing to do with the fact that she'd spent part of her evening surfing the web for more on Constantine Zimin.

Mimi had been right when she'd said there was little to find in the way of personal information.

But he was pretty. Boy, was he pretty. Even more so in person.

And so, yes, her dreams had been…interesting. Images of dueling tongues and tangled limbs had left a thin sheen of moisture between her skin and her sleep shorts.

She'd watched a few of Zimin's highlight videos on YouTube and found him to be graceful on the ice, in a lethal sort of way. Suji had never paid much attention to hockey but could see the appeal. There was aggression, for sure, but it was calculated. Targeted. And Zimin was apparently one of the best at what he did. She still didn't like that, in a few hours, he'd likely bring hordes of reporters with cameras to the hospital. Her attempts to derail the debacle had fallen on deaf ears.

Suji showered, threw on her pink scrubs, the ones with the unicorn print, and headed out. By the time she stepped out of the elevator and into her ward, it was eight on the nose.

"Morning, boss lady."

""Hey, Tim. How was the night?" Suji spoke around the maple walnut scone she'd grabbed from the coffee shop downstairs. She really needed to start eating better.

Tim smiled. "Not bad. Aaron had a little trouble breathing, but it was an issue with his oxygen. The unit's been replaced, so all is good."

Suji frowned. "That's the second time this month something's gone wrong with one of those things."

"It happens."

"Not this often. I'll have to talk to their rep. It's an Emerson, isn't it?"

"Yeah," Tim nodded. "The 4500."

"Thanks." Suji pulled out her phone to leave herself a memo. "Are you heading out?"

"Not yet," Tim replied. "Mimi said she'd be a little late today. Something about a hair appointment this morning."

"Geez, thanks for covering for her. Go get yourself some coffee or something, I'm here."

"You rock, thanks."

Suji went to her office to hang up her jacket, waving to the others on staff as she passed. Someone knocked on the open door, and she turned to find Dr. Morris standing there.

"Morning, Suji. Got a sec?"

"Sure, Calvin, come on in."

He stepped inside and closed the door. "I wanted to talk to you before the event later this morning."

"I'm still not happy about it."

"Believe me, you've made your position quite clear." Calvin smiled. "But Mr. Zimin and his team have big plans, plans that will only help us serve our patients better."

"What sort of plans?"

Calvin cleared his throat as he took the seat in front of her desk.

Suji sat in her chair, curious.

"This information doesn't leave this room," Calvin insisted.

"Of course."

"Zimin is working to establish a foundation to assist families with children undergoing long-term care."

Suji narrowed her eyes. "What sort of assistance?"

"Some would be monetary, helping them to travel here for treatment, I'm not privy to all of the details. Regardless, we weren't about to say no to the man's help."

"It sounds like a nice idea." Suji sat back. "You trust that he's serious about it?"

"Very. His sister was a patient here when they were kids."

"Really?" She hadn't seen anything about that in her snooping. Then again, there had been very little about him at all online.

"Yeah, he's very private about it, so please don't bring it up unless he does."

"Me? I won't have occasion to talk to the man."

Calvin smiled. "Suji, I need you to play nice today. I know you feel protective of our kids, but really. It's going to be all right. Zim has hired an entertainer for them."

"Zim?"

Calvin shrugged one shoulder. "He insisted."

Zim sounded so much more…something….than Con. Suji suppressed a shiver.

"What sort of entertainer?"

"A magician, I believe he said. And, of course, there will be a professional photographer to take photos of the kids with The Cup, if they want one."

Suji bristled. "This is exactly what I was afraid of. Photos? Who gave him, or us for that matter, permission to use these kids as props? Are you going to call their parents and ask them to sign release forms?"

"Suji…"

She shook her head. "No, Calvin, this is why I didn't want that guy and his entourage anywhere near my ward."

"Your ward?" Calvin arched an eyebrow.

"Fine." She acquiesced. "I suppose you know what you're doing, being the head of the department and all."

Calvin laughed. "I really enjoy working with you, Nurse Meriwether."

Suji smiled. "Me too, Dr. Morris. But if I see things getting out of hand today, I'm putting a stop to it."

"If things get out of hand today, I'll put a stop to it myself," Calvin reassured her.

"A foundation, huh?"

Calvin nodded. "Yep, or so the paperwork says."

She'd believe it when she saw it.

***

Suji had just administered medicine to one of her patients when she stepped out of the room and slammed right into a hard body. Strong hands kept her from falling to the hard, tiled floor.

"Fuck."

"Dammit."

"I'm so sorry, I didn't see you coming out."

"No, I..." Suji blinked up at Constantine Zimin, her apology dying in her throat.

He was even taller than she'd remembered. His eyes were warm, like chocolate lava cake, and his hair a mop of chestnut on top his head. He was dressed in his team's jersey, the logo a bright, green alligator who apparently spent a ton of time in the gym.

"Uh...no-no problem."

Zimin smiled. "Nurse Meriwether, eh?"

Suji blinked again, realizing he still had his hands around her upper arms. And were his thumbs gently caressing her, or was that her caffeine-deprived imagination? She eased back, and he released her.

"Y-yes."

"Constantine Zimin."

"Er, nice to formally meet you, Mr. Zimin.

His smile was warm too. "I think it's safe for you to call me Zim."

"Not Con?"

"Not Sue?"

"Fair enough, Zim it is. I'm sorry if my initial welcome wasn't more, uh, welcoming. To be honest, I was a little freaked out."

"It's all right. I understand. If someone I'd…met in a bar the night before showed up at my job, I'd be freaked out too.

A tiny smile threatened to curve her lips. "I bet."

"And I wanted to reassure you that I only have the best intentions where your patients, and the department, are concerned. I just want to help."

Suji nodded and smiled, the initial shock of seeing him having worn off. "I'm glad to hear it. Dr. Morris tells me you're setting up some sort of foundation."

"Yeah, though there won't be any sort of public announcement until tonight. I'm holding a fundraiser."

"I see." Suji started walking, and Zim fell into step alongside her. "What drove you to do it, found the organization?"

"My sister was a patient here some years back."

"Oh?"

"She was diagnosed when we were children," he continued.

"Will she be involved in your charity?" Suji stopped to sign some paperwork at the desk.

"No," Zim's tone took on a bit of gravel. "She died when we were seventeen."

Suji's breath caught. Without thinking, she placed her hand on his forearm.

"You were twins? I'm so sorry, I didn't know."

He gave her a small nod. "It isn't public knowledge. You couldn't have known."

Suji studied him. Up close, he was a sobering sight. Gorgeous, yes, but also severe. She found herself imagining what sort of lover he'd be. Attentive and focused were the words that came to mind, followed by the thought *why the hell am I wondering what he'd be like in bed when he just told me he lost his sister?* The desire to comfort him had arisen in her so fast, she could barely breathe.

Quickly, she removed her hand.

Zim smiled. "This isn't awkward at all."

Suji chuckled. "Sorry, you just caught me off-guard."

"Something tells me that doesn't happen very often. And I get the feeling you don't like it."

"Not normally, no." She felt herself smiling, and Zim returned it. They fell into a bubble of silence that seemed to stretch and grow.

"Hey, Zim."

A big, burly man with mahogany skin and big, black eyes stepped up to them.

"Oh, hey Tony." He shook the man's hand. "Tony, this is Nurse Meriwether. Nurse Meriwether, this is Tony."

"Miss." Tony shook her hand before turning back to Zim. "Motz wants to know where to set up The Cup."

Zim nodded toward Suji. "She's in charge around here."

"I think the game room is best," she replied.

"I know where it is, I can show you." Zim smiled at her, and something fluttered in her stomach. "I'm sure Ms. Meriwether has plenty to do. Let's not get in her hair, lovely as it is."

Wait. Was he flirting with her?

Before she could react, Zim and Tony headed back toward the elevator. A few minutes later, they returned with two other men. One was almost as big as Tony, with closely cropped blond hair and an unfortunate goatee. The other was small, wiry, and around fifty years old. He rushed to keep up, and kept pushing his too-big glasses up the bridge of his nose and swiping his dark brown hair out of his eyes. Between them, the two larger men wheeled an enormous black case. It was big enough to hold a small adult.

Or even a large child, Suji thought, eyeing the thing. She'd have to make sure none of the kids climbed inside.

The three men headed toward the game room, Zim leading the way. Suji trailed behind, watching with fascination as Zim moved. Having seen him on the dance floor, she noted that he was equally sexy off of it. This was a dangerous thought.

No matter how philanthropic, sympathetic, and charming he may seem, he was still a pro athlete. Not exactly marriage material.

Marriage?

What the hell had they put in her coffee this morning? Suji was never one to daydream about white picket fences and two-point-five children. She was the de facto mother to hundreds of kids over the course of a year. But one makeout sesh with a hockey player, and she was having wet dreams and Martha Stewart fantasies.

Seriously, what the hell?

Maybe it was how good his hands felt when he grabbed her arms to keep her from falling, or the cheeky grin he'd given her. Or the dozen inebriated kisses they'd shared. Whatever it was, she needed to get her head back on straight. Fast.

"Excuse me, miss?" The wiry man walked over to her.

"Yes?"

"Is there somewhere we can stash the case? I don't want to leave it for the kids to injure themselves."

"Of course, Mr…"

"Motz, but call me Eddie."

"Eddie, I'm Suji. I'm happy to have it placed in storage. Tell me, though, how many reporters are you expecting here today?"

"Oh, well, I'm not in charge of the press coverage. That's Zim's team. Speaking of which, I think his agent is on the way. You could ask him. My only job is keeping The Cup safe."

"Really?" She chuckled. "Safe from what?"

"Damage, mostly." Eddie removed his glasses and proceeded to clean them with a square of black cloth that seemed to appear out of nowhere. "You'd be surprised what some of the players get up to with their twenty-four hours."

Suji frowned. "Twenty-four hours?"

"Each player on The Cup-winning team gets twenty-four hours with it, as does the coach, some other members of the coaching staff and some management."

"Oh, I see."

That Zim had chosen to spend part of his day at the hospital melted just a little bit of the ice around her heart.

"Zim actually gets it a bit longer, since he's the last to have The Cup before I take it back to Toronto." Eddie replaced his glasses and tucked the cloth away in his pocket. "I got in last evening, and I don't fly out again until early tomorrow."

Suji nodded. "I bet you've seen some crazy stuff, then. With The Cup and the players, I mean."

Eddie nodded. "You have no idea. Maybe someday I'll write a book," he snickered. "I love my job, though. Guys like Zim make it easier. We have this event for the kids, and a fundraiser of some sort tonight. I'm not sure what he has planned in the interim, but I doubt there will be any wild parties. Besides, that's not his reputation."

"Do you know him well?" She couldn't help but ask.

"Only via league hearsay. From that, he seems like a stand-up guy."

Suji nodded. "Well, that's nice."

"Anyway, if you'll point me in the direction of your storage room, I'll be out of your way."

CHAPTER 8

ZIM'S AGENT was not a happy man.

"No television?"

"Nope."

"At all?" The man was actually whining.

"None."

Marty Kohn sighed like he had the weight of the world on his shoulders.

"Why do you insist on making my job so god-damned difficult?"

"Watch your language, this is a children's' ward."

Marty held up his hands in apology. "Sorry, I just…I'm trying to get you another endorsement deal."

"Which I don't need or want."

"Yeah, yeah." Marty waved him off. "You say that, but if I put a contract worth five mil in front of you, you'd sign it in a New York minute."

"Excuse me," a very young, very blond, very pretty woman in nursing scrubs interrupted. "Are you Subzero?"

Ugh. As if the jersey and the big shiny trophy hadn't given it away.

"Uh, yeah."

Her eyes brightened as she turned to wave over two other young women, both equally attractive. The taller one had smooth skin, the color of sorrel, with sharp cheekbones and a wicked smile. The other was a redhead with fair, freckled skin and ice blue eyes. All three women presented a nice picture, but the predatory gleam in their eyes was all too familiar.

"We were wondering if we could take a selfie with you."

Fuck no. "Um…"

"He'd be happy to," Marty answered for him. "Anything for his fans. Right, Subzero?"

"I'm from New Orleans," the brunette offered, sidling up to Zim. "My dad is a big Rage fan, and I am too."

"Cool." Her tits were fans too, apparently, since she kept pushing them against his side.

She snaked one arm around his waist and smiled as she stuck out the other, long, bony arm, her camera in hand.

Zim attempted what he hoped was a smile as she snapped a few photos. Her friends then took turns doing the same, and Zim tried not to let on how much he hated it. Social media was a menace, as far as he was concerned, and he avoided it at all costs.

"Thank you," the blond purred, going up on tiptoe to plant a sloppy kiss on his cheek. Her perfume was a cloying mixture of flowers and baby powder.

"Sure."

The trio giggled, heads-down over their phones as they walked away. Zim looked up in time to see Suji, her expression sour. Great. She turned and walked briskly in the other direction.

Out of the corner of his eye, Zim caught sight of a shady looking dude with a camera. He wore a press pass, so he was probably legit, but there was something about him that set off alarm bells.

"Who is that guy?"

Marty turned to follow Zim's line of sight. "Oh, that's Craig Bannon from the Inquirer. He wants to interview you, get a few shots of you with the kids."

Zim shook his head. "I'm fine with a short interview, but absolutely no shots of the kids. Not with me and not without the parents' permission, or the hospital's. Marty, you know the rules."

"Yeah, but I thought we could ask. It would look great for you to be seen…"

"No. Fuck!" Zim tried to temper the rage in his voice. Marty was a decent guy, as agents went, but he'd never hesitate to play an angle. "Just…no."

"Fine, fine." Marty raised his hands in surrender. "But about that endorsement deal…"

Zim groaned. "Not everything is about money, Marty. And I already make more than I can spend."

"But you won't play forever. Look at what happened to Jonas."

The low growl that emanated from Zim's throat made Marty take a step back.

"I only meant that you have to start thinking about your future. What about your wife and kids? Don't you want to provide for them?"

"Wife and kids?"

"Theoretically."

"Of course, but…"

"And what about this here charity thing?" Marty continued. "You need money for that."

He had a point. "Who wants to offer me five million, and for what?"

"MacroMuscle," Marty supplied. "It's a sports supplement."

"Never heard of it."

"Yeah, well, no one has. That's why they want you to be their spokesperson."

Zim snorted. "Why would I endorse something I've never heard of, much less have ever used."

Marty stuck a hand into his briefcase and pulled out a stack of papers, shuffling through them until he found whatever he was looking for.

"The product is all-natural, all of the ingredients are sourced here in the U.S., and the company's owner is a big Rage fan."

"I don't know, Marty." Zim ran a hand through his hair.

On the other side of the room, some of the patients and their parents had started to gather around The Cup. The photographer he'd hired, a kid right out of Penn Arts University, had set up lighting and a neutral backdrop to give each visitor a nice souvenir to take home. A few of the nurses had already taken their photos. There had been no sign of Tiffany or little Aaron, and Zim wondered if they had been discharged.

"Just think about it, Zim." Marty insisted. "You could donate the entire fee to your little charity thing if you wanted. Minus my cut, of course," he added.

"Yeah, sure," Zim agreed. "I'll think about it."

"Great, great." Marty smiled with apparent relief. "Listen, can we take a quick shot of us with The Cup? I've got to get going."

"Sure."

After Marty had left, Zim realized he hadn't eaten anything in hours. His body was a well-oiled machine that consumed a crazy amount of calories. He had to constantly refuel, or he'd get tired and cranky.

He ducked out of the game room to find the cafeteria, where he grabbed a turkey sandwich – which he scarfed down before even finished paying for it – and a couple of bananas. He'd just swallowed the last bit of the fruit when he spotted Suji.

She had her head over what appeared to be a patient's chart. Judging by her clothing, the woman standing next to her was a doctor. Zim watched the exchange, fascinated by the petite brunette.

There was an air of authority to her, like she wouldn't take shit from anyone, no matter who they were. But at the same time, Zim sensed a carefully guarded vulnerability. The duality intrigued him, and he wondered again if it would be too crazy to ask her out. He hadn't intended to bring a date to the fundraiser, but for her, he'd change his plans. He'd had a small taste of her, and it hadn't been nearly enough.

She was gorgeous, even with minimal make-up and wrinkled scrubs the color of Pepto Bismol, covered in cartoon unicorns. He'd met so many women who put their appearance above everything else that he found Suji refreshing.

Zim had been so busy staring at her that he hadn't noticed she was staring right back. He straightened, trying to think of a way to cover.

Suji and the doctor parted ways, and she made her way over to him.

"Did you need something, Mr. Zimin?"

Zim already knew how this scenario would play out, but he went for it anyway.

"Have dinner with me."

The expression on Suji's face would have been comical if it weren't directed at him. Her eyes, as gorgeous as they were, were cold as freshly laid ice.

"I have a better idea," she said in a voice like the darkest hot chocolate. "Why don't you find one of those young nursing students to keep you company tonight. They seemed pretty eager to become a notch on a hockey star's belt."

Ouch.

"Assuming, of course, there's still room on that belt." She continued and let out a laugh as tart as fresh lemonade. "What am I saying? You could always buy another. I'm sure you have one in every color."

If looks could kill, Zim was sure hers would have fitted him with cement shoes and sent him sinking to the bottom of the Schuylkill River.

Zim chuckled. He really did like this woman. "Look, Nurse Meriwether."

"Her name is Suji," a small voice chimed. Tiffany peered around an open door, her green eyes flashing. Great. Not only was Zim about to be rejected, but it would happen in front of a precocious preteen.

"Tiffany…" Suji's demeanor did a complete one-eighty as she turned from him and gave her full attention to her young patient. "You don't volunteer personal information like that to strangers."

"But he's not a stranger," young Tiffany protested as Suji walked into her room. "He's Subzero."

Zim followed close behind, though he knew he probably shouldn't. It was just that Suji's transformation from annoyance to profound and genuine concern, wrapped up as it was in a blanket of easy smiles, intrigued him beyond measure. He watched as she drew back the curtain that had blocked the view of the bed from the door and cupped the young girl's face, a face that brightened even more with the contact.

The sight tugged at Zim's heartstrings. But all the machinery surrounding the young girl brought him up short.

When he'd met Tiffany the day before, she'd been so energetic. Forceful, even. Aside from the pale, matching hospital gowns over their pajamas, she and Aaron had just looked like two kids arguing over a video game. Seeing Tiffany hooked up to the machines that surrounded her bed seemed wrong on so many levels.

Zim cleared the tight regret from his throat. "Heya, Tiff."

Her mouth was two-teeth short of a full smile. "Hey."

He winked and offered what he hoped was a reassuring grin.

There were so many things beeping, so many lines of thin plastic tubing snaking their way toward her little body, Zim couldn't find his breath. It reminded him too much of his sister, Mila. He took a step back from the bed. Then another. And another, until he was clear of the sight of her, though he could still hear the *ping ping ping* of her heartbeat monitor.

Zim found himself standing next to an empty waiting room at the other end of the ward. Grateful for the solitude, he sat on the edge of the unforgiving chair. He wasn't sure how long he sat there before a familiar voice roused him from his thoughts.

"A-are you alright?"

He glanced up to find little Aaron standing in front of him, his expression filled with concern.

"I'm fine," he croaked.

Aaron moved closer. The bitter smell of antiseptic fought for dominance over the delicate scent of fabric softener as he sat down next to him. The hand he placed on Zim's knee was warm, and Zim hadn't realized how much he needed the touch.

"Did you lose somebody?"

Zim nodded. Of course, he'd recognize the signs. "My sister."

"I'm sorry." Aaron's voice, so filled with sympathy, had Zim fighting back tears he hadn't shed in almost a decade. He managed to grind out a thank you and forced a smile.

Zim heard something, a mechanical clicking. Like a camera shutter. He turned toward the noise, but couldn't place the source.

"Hey there," Suji appeared in the doorway. "What's this, a conspiracy?" She smiled as she walked into the room.

"Subzero is sad," Aaron offered, mournfully.

"I'm okay, buddy." Zim took a deep breath and forced what he hoped was a more convincing smile. "Just memories, that's all."

"Aaron, how about you let Subzero have a few minutes before he comes out for the autographs and photos?" Suji patted the young boy lightly on the shoulder, and he stood.

"Okay." He shuffled toward the door, his I.V. pole in tow. "But if you need to talk, I can talk to you."

Zim thought he might start bawling any minute. "Thanks, buddy. I'll be right there. Hold the fort for me, okay?"

Aaron brightened. "I'm in charge until you get there?"

"That's right," Zim replied, not needing to force a smile this time.

As Aaron disappeared from sight, Suji sat in his place.

"How old was she?" Suji's voice was softer than he'd ever heard it, with an almost musical quality.

"We'd just turned seventeen."

Her hand found his and squeezed. "You're serious about wanting to do this thing for the kids?"

Zim met her eyes, nodding. "There's a lot that I want to do, plans I want to make, I-"

"Okay, then," she interrupted. "Yes."

"Huh?"

A soft smile curved her full lips. "I'll have dinner with you, and then you can tell me all about it."

***

Had she really just agreed to go out with a hockey star?

"You did what?" Mimi sounded as astonished as Suji felt.

"I told him I'd have dinner with him."

"Shit, girl. You go from zero to sixty like that, huh?"

"It's not like that," Suji argued. "There's a fundraiser tonight, and I agreed to go with him. He's going to fill me in on some foundation that he's starting."

Mimi pursed her lips. "Sweetheart, who are you trying to fool? You haven't stopped looking at that yummy slice of beefcake since he stepped into the game room."

She wasn't wrong. Suji hadn't been able to stop staring, not after she found him sitting with Aaron. Talking with Aaron. Aaron, who never spoke to anyone. He was one of the kids in the ward whose parents were unable to stay with him full-time. Instead, they traveled back and forth on weekends to visit.

"He's nothing like I expected."

Mimi nodded. "I'll give you that. The Nursettes tried their siren song on him earlier, and he didn't even bat an eye in their direction."

"Yeah, I saw that. I need to have a chat with the head of Teaching."

"You do that," Mimi fumed. "It was downright embarrassing. I'm glad there aren't any television cameras covering this."

"No kidding," Suji acknowledged, glad Zim had kept his promise.

Overall, the event was going well. The kids were thrilled, and the parents seemed happy too. A couple of them appeared to know who Zim was, and he accommodated them with photos and autographs. The few reporters that had come were respectful of the children, all except for one.

"Did security escort the asshole Bannon out the front door?"

Mimi nodded. "Yeah, they tossed him out on his rear. The nerve of him, trying to interview some of the kids without their parents' permission. Or ours."

Suji nodded. "Some people have no morals."

"None," Mimi agreed.

A loud laugh from the corner of the game room caught Suji's attention. She looked up to find Zim crouched down in front of Aaron who was animatedly describing something to him, his hands flying.

"Well, look at that," Mimi mused. "I've never seen little Aaron so engaged, not unless his dad is here for a visit, or Tiffany drags a conversation out of him."

"I know." Suji crossed her arms and leaned against the counter, content to watch the pair. "I found them chatting earlier and couldn't believe it."

Mimi nudged her shoulder. "Watch yourself, doll."

Suji frowned. "Why?"

"Yesterday, you were hell bent on keeping this guy out of our ward," she remarked. "And today, you're looking at him with stars in your eyes."

Suji sniffed. "No, I am not."

"Uh, yeah you are, and I do not blame you one bit. He's been sneaking glances at you too."

Suji spun to face her. "Really?"

Mimi chuckled. "Yep, like right now."

Suji's heart rate ticked up. "He's looking right now?"

"Sizing you up like a three-course meal."

"Shit."

"Breathe, girl." Mimi laughed.

"What was I thinking, agreeing to have dinner with him?"

"You were thinking 'what a nice guy, who is also hot as fuck,' that's what you were thinking."

Suji gaped at Mimi and whispered. "You're a dirty girl."

"You ain't lying," Mimi said, laughing harder.

"Seriously, though," Suji whined. "What am I going to do?"

Mimi squared her shoulders, looking Suji in the eye. "Jokes aside, I'm glad to see you do something other than come here, work yourself to death, only to go home to an empty apartment, eat take-out and collapse in a heap."

Not an inaccurate description of Suji's daily routine.

"You didn't agree to marry the guy," Mimi reminded her. "You're just going to a fancy dinner with a good-looking man. It's for a good cause, and it's something you can tell your grandkids someday."

"You're right."

"I know I am," Mimi agreed. "Now, what are you going to wear to this fancy schmancy fundraiser?"

Suji blanched. "Crap, I have shit for clothes in that department."

"Maybe you should hit Amrita up for something," Mimi suggested. "That sister of yours is a fashion horse."

"True." Suji fished her phone out of her pocket. "That's a great idea."

"I'm full of them today," Mimi joked.

CHAPTER 9

SUJI WAS BEGINNING to regret calling her sister.

"I look like a prostitute."

"A very high-end prostitute," Amrita countered.

"Do you actually wear this in public?" Suji tugged at the hem of the sleek, black shift which barely covered her ass. "Seriously, where's the rest of it?"

Amrita giggled. "Okay, so maybe this isn't your style. Try the yellow one."

"No way, I look jaundiced in yellow."

"True," her sister agreed. ""Maybe the Tadashi Shoji?"

The red, cocktail dress was gorgeous, its lacy bodice timelessly elegant. Sexy, sheer sleeves and a deep-V back added just enough allure to keep it from being too matronly.

Tossing the black barely-a-dress onto the growing pile of clothes on her bed, Suji gingerly picked up the wine-colored sheath.

"How much was this?"

Her sister shook her head. "Don't worry about that, put it on."

The silky material felt heavenly against her skin, such a contrast to the rough cotton of her everyday scrubs. Suji smoothed the skirt down over her legs.

"Wow."

"Yeah?"

"Oh, yeah," Amrita said, admiringly. "He won't know what hit him."

"Amri, I'm not going to snag a man, I'm going to help the hospital."

"Two birds, one stone," Amrita teased. "Or look me in the eye and tell me you aren't the least bit curious about what that hunk of a man looks like underneath all those clothes."

"I'm beginning to regret telling you anything about this."

"Hey, I wasn't the one sucking face with him at the bar the other night."

"Ugh, that was a mistake."

"And I wasn't the one who whipped out the laptop and showed me sexy pics of your hockey stud."

"Another mistake," Suji remarked as she eyed her reflection in her floor-length mirror. "I think this dress'll do."

"You think?" Amrita clambered off the bed and over to where Suji stood. "You look amazing."

"Hair down or up?"

"Down. I love this new bob thing you have going on. Very sassy."

"Thanks." Suji turned toward her bathroom to finish putting on her makeup.

Amrita followed, leaning against the doorframe. She smiled at Suji's reflection in the bathroom mirror.

"I'm proud of you."

Suji laughed. "For what?"

"For putting yourself out there."

"Amri, I told you, this isn't a date," Suji insisted, trying hard to convince herself of that fact.

"I know it's not the first of many, but it is a date, judging by how nervous you are."

"It's just been a while since I spent time around this many adults, not to mention adults with deep pockets who could do a lot of good for THUP."

"Will Calvin be there?"

"Yeah, along with most of the board."

"See? Nothing to worry about, then. It's their job to wine and dine the donors. All you have to do is be arm candy for the sports star."

Suji paused, right in the middle of applying her lipstick, and gave her sister the evil eye.

"What the hell, Amri?"

Amrita snorted. "Jesus, I'm kidding. Look at your face!"

"I will smack you."

The doorbell rang.

Amrita arched an eyebrow. "He's picking you up here?"

"He insisted."

"He's early."

Too early. Suji wasn't nearly ready for this. Was it too late to cancel?

"Breathe," Amrita ordered as she made her way to the front door.

Suji tried to use a few calming methods to even out her breaths. She was counting back from ten when Amrita returned with an enormous bouquet of orchids and a shit-eating grin.

"What were you saying about it not being a date?"

"Those are stunning." Suji took the vase from her and walked toward the kitchen.

"There's a card," Amrita announced before snatching it from the top of the arrangement.

Looking forward to the pleasure of your company this evening.
A car will pick you up at seven.
Yours, Z

"How very formal," Amrita noted. "And he's sending a car? Why not come get you himself?"

Suji set the vase on her kitchen counter and tried to tamp down her disappointment.

"I told you it wasn't a date, Amri. I'll meet him at the restaurant, have dinner, schmooze with the well-heeled crowd, and be home before the carriage turns into a pumpkin."

"You do realize that, in that metaphor, you get to kiss the prince," Amrita smirked.

"Nah, I'm not cut out to be a princess."

"Hey, if the Manolo pump fits."

CHAPTER 10

ZIM LOVED HOCKEY. He loved everything about the game. The ice, the speed, the feel of flying from one end of the rink to the other. And it was like flying, or as close as he'd ever come to it.

He loved his team, they had heart. Their manager had integrity and knew the game inside and out. Zim loved it all. But he hated this part.

This was the very worst part, the cameras and the handshakes and the disingenuous questions. He could have done without any of it.

"Hey, Subzero, over here!"

Zim turned toward the photographer, pushed his hair out of his eyes, and forced his lips to curve upward. He hoped it at least approximated a smile. He kept telling himself it was for a good cause. Pose for a few photos with the right people, and wallets would open.

"Just a few more minutes, Zim, and then you can relax and have a few drinks."

Zim's agent had a difficult job. Not only did he have to deal with a client that all but refused to be photographed out of uniform, but said client was also hesitant to sign a five-million-dollar endorsement deal that would put seven-hundred-fifty-thousand dollars in his own pocket.

"I'm fine, Marty. Any sign of my parents?"

The agent checked his very expensive watch. "The car picked them up half-an-hour ago, they should be here any minute."

"Good, thanks for arranging that. And the other car?"

Marty grinned. "She's on her way too."

"Thanks."

Marty kept grinning.

Zim tried to ignore him.

"What?"

"You invited a woman to an event."

Zim sniffed. "So? It's not the first time."

"Actually," Marty countered, his thick black eyebrows high on his forehead. "It is, to my knowledge."

"She's the Head Nurse in Pediatrics, and I thought she should be here."

Marty nodded. "Right, I get that, but you invited her here as your date."

"I didn't."

"Yeah, you did," Marty stated. "It's good to see."

"Meaning?"

"Zim, you are one of the hottest bachelors in sports, let alone hockey. People ask me all the time, is he seeing anyone? Is he straight? Gay?"

Zim fumed. "Who the fuck's business is it what I do with my personal life?"

"No one's," Marty acknowledged. "No one god-damned person's. But here's the thing, people are curious creatures. And a guy that looks like you, has your money, and your career, they're going to wonder and ask and speculate."

"They can speculate all they want. Even if I were seeing someone, I sure as shit wouldn't want it all over the sports news and tabloid websites."

"Lydia and I would make sure to keep any mention of your love life out of the news," Marty assured him.

Zim's publicist, Lydia Valtersen, was a vital part of his team. She'd done a stellar job keeping the details of his private life private.

"I appreciate the sentiment, Marty, but there's nothing to mention."

Marty grinned again. "At the moment."

"Oh, look. My parents are here."

Zim was grateful for the interruption and quickly made his way over to the front door of the restaurant.

The Manayunk, located in the belly of a large tall ship, served nouveau American cuisine in a retro-roaring twenties atmosphere. The vessel itself was permanently moored on the Delaware River, boasted a five-star menu, and had a spectacular view of center city Philadelphia. The interior consisted of warm, worn oak and rich red velvet.

Zim watched as his mother took it all in. This was definitely right up her alley, and he kicked himself for not bringing her here before now.

"Mama." Zim took her hands and leaned down to kiss her cheeks. She wore a simple, mint green shift in soft chiffon.

"Kolya," she breathed. "This is beautiful."

"I knew you'd like it," Zim replied, smiling. "And you look lovely."

Zim's father helped her out of her coat and handed it to the hostess before shedding his own.

"Very nice," Gennady remarked, wearing a dark navy suit and a tie that matched Lilya's dress. "Reminds me a little of the homeland."

Lilya nodded. "Yes, the wood and the colors, very…what's the word? Opulesce?"

"Opulent," Zim supplied.

"Yes," she beamed. "That's it."

"I have a table for you over by a window, so you can see the river." Zim led them to the spot.

"Are we not sitting with you?"

"I'll be close by, Mama. I have…someone joining me for dinner."

Lilya stopped, her hand on his arm gripped him tight. "A girl?"

"Yes, but…"

"Oh, Kolya!" His mother clapped her hands together lightly. "It's about time."

"Mama…"

"Is she here yet? We want to meet her, don't we, Genya?"

Zim's father nodded, smiling at Zim over her head. "Of course we would, Lilechka, but something tells me Kolya's not quite ready."

"It's not a date, mom. She's on staff at the hospital."

"Is she very pretty?"

Zim pulled out a chair for his mother, and she lowered herself into it. His father took the chair on the other side of the table.

"Yes, mama, she is."

Well, he couldn't very well lie to his mother. Suji Meriwether was a beautiful woman.

"Well," she replied, beaming. "You never know where you will find your soulmate. Your father and I met when he delivered milk to our family's house."

Zim frowned, smiling. "You never told me that."

His father nodded. "We did."

"I thought you met in school."

"We were in the same school," his father confirmed. "But we were in different years. I didn't know her before the day I dropped a jug of milk on their walkway."

"Glass and milk went everywhere. My father was so angry," Lilya provided, chuckling. "But I told him to go away, and I dealt with Genya myself."

"You told *dedushka* to go away?" Zim laughed at the notion. His grandfather had been very much the disciplinarian, although he always had a soft spot for Zim's mother.

"I did," she replied with a mischievous grin. "I thought your father was too cute to be subjected to your grandfather's wrath. He probably would have had him fired."

"But your mother convinced him to let me replace the milk."

"Yes. I hopped on the back of his bicycle and Genya cycled us all the way back to the dairy farm. Together, we brought back a fresh jug."

"And that was that," his father stated, smiling lovingly at his wife.

"Yes." Lilya reached across the table and took his hand. "That was that."

Zim had always admired his parents, their devotion to each other and to their children. And even though he knew they loved each other very much, it wasn't often displayed which such open affection.

"This is what we want for you, Kolya," his mother turned her shining eyes on him. "Love is a powerful compass. When you have it, it can guide you along your path."

"He'll find someone in his own time, Lilichka."

She nodded at his father's words. "I know. But only if he keeps his eyes open. Take that young lady over there." She pointed behind Zim. "She is lovely, isn't she? With kind eyes."

Zim turned to find Suji standing at the front of the restaurant.

She smiled when she spotted him, her hand lifting slightly with a wave. She looked…incredible.

Her hair fell to the tops of her shoulders in soft waves, and she'd put on a little make-up. Nothing to overpower her luminous skin, but her lips were the color of dark cherries, and Zim had to lick his own.

The urge to kiss her roared up out of nowhere.

Zim couldn't take his eyes off her as she made her way over to him. It was only when she stopped that he realized his parents had still been talking.

"Sorry I'm late," Suji offered.

"No, you're…you're not late. Um…" Words? What were words?

Out of the corner of his eye, Zim saw his father stand up. "Aren't you going to introduce us?"

"Uh, yeah," Zim sputtered. "Of course. Papa, this is Sujarta Meriwether, Head Nurse in Pediatrics at The Hospital of the University of Philadelphia. Suji, these are my parents, Lilya and Gennady Zimin."

Suji extended her hand to his mother. "A pleasure, Mrs. Zimin."

Zim chanced a glance at his mother and found her absolutely beaming, utterly mesmerized by Suji. He couldn't blame her, she looked like she'd stepped out of a magazine.

"It is so lovely to meet you, Suji."

"Our son speaks very highly of you," Zim's father marveled when Suji offered her hand to him.

"Does he? I'm sure he's prone to exaggeration."

"Our Constantine? Never." His father chuckled.

Suji smiled, and it was teasing and playful. Zim hadn't seen this side of her, and he found that he liked it very much. Maybe too much.

"Well, he made quite an impression on my kids today."

Lilya's face fell. "Oh, you are married?"

Way to be subtle, mama, Zim thought.

"Oh! No, Mrs. Zimin."

"She meant the children in her ward, mama."

Just like that, the light returned to her eyes. He would have to have a chat with his mother later.

"Oh, good."

Suji's brows knit together, but she smiled.

"I-I didn't mean good, I meant," his mother floundered. "Excuse me, my English is not so good."

Zim stifled a laugh.

His father, on the other hand, did not. He took his seat, shaking his head and cackling to himself.

"Please excuse my wife, she is a hopeless romantic."

"Aren't we all," Suji replied, still smiling.

Zim made a mental note of that fact too.

"Mama, papa, we're going to find our table and leave you to it. Enjoy yourselves, *da*?"

His mother grabbed his forearm and pulled.

Zim bent over, and she cupped his cheek, turning his head.

"You really like her," she whispered.

"I just met her, mama," Zim whispered back.

She released him and caught his eye, her expression full of mischief.

"So, go get to know her better." She winked.

Fortunately, Suji had been occupied by another guest.

Zim joined her. When she was done, he offered his arm, which she took.

He'd chosen a table at the other end of the ship, away from the bulk of the partygoers. This way, he could put in the requisite time with them, and retreat when he needed to.

"This is pretty far from the action, isn't it?" Suji noted.

"By design."

"Want me all to yourself do you?" She was still teasing, but Zim saw something else in her eyes. Uncertainty.

He was right there with her. He couldn't deny the attraction, but he wasn't sure what they were doing at this point. He had no game plan.

Instead of answering, he offered to pour her some wine. "Red or white?"

"In this dress, I'm safe with red."

Zim raised an eyebrow.

"I'm a clutz when it comes to any sort of fancy dress. I can tap a vein with my eyes closed, hook up a drip in seconds, but put me in a dress? I'm Drew Barrymore in *Never Been Kissed*." Suji grinned.

Zim hadn't seen the film, but he got the gist of it. "Red it is. And the dress is beautiful, by the way."

Was that a blush on her cheeks? "Thanks. I borrowed it from my sister. She's into clothes and all that."

Zim filled her glass and then his own. "And you're not?"

"I don't have much occasion for street clothes. But I own about a hundred different sets of scrubs, in every conceivable color and pattern."

Zim chuckled. "I liked the unicorns."

"Yeah?" She smiled and took a sip of her wine. "I'm partial to those myself. And the kids love them."

"Hey," Zim started. "How is Tiffany?"

Suji's expression sobered. "She's actually okay. She had chemo this morning, and she sometimes reacts badly. That's why she wasn't at the party today."

"Ah."

"But she's been responding really well to treatment. We have every confidence she'll beat this thing."

"That is fantastic news."

Suji's smile was a mixture of pride and relief. "It is."

They sat in silence for a few awkward moments. Zim racked his brain for a topic of conversation that didn't revolve around her work.

"Tell me about your sport," Suji said, rescuing him. "I confess, I know nothing about it. When did you start playing?"

If there was one thing Zim could talk about, ad nauseum, it was hockey.

"My father strapped my sister and I both into skates as soon as we could walk. We lived near the Ice Palace in St. Petersburg."

"Oh," Suji said. "I didn't know you were born in Russia. How old were you when you moved to the United States?"

"Ten." Thankfully, she didn't ask why, so Zim continued. "Anyway, my father played hockey before he met my mother, so he's always been in love with the sport. He passed that on to me."

"And what do you love about it?" Suji watched him with glittering, amber eyes.

Zim kept getting caught in that mysterious gaze.

"The speed, the skills you need to develop, the discipline," Zim answered without thinking. "I love the camaraderie with my teammates. Unlike some other sports, it's never a one-man show. One player hardly ever carries a whole team."

"You have to work as a unit."

"Yeah, that's it exactly."

"Not so different from my and my team," Suji remarked. "Not one of us could do the job alone. We work together to make sure each child has the care they need."

Zim nodded. "Yeah, you're right. My teammates and I work together toward our target, scoring goals, winning games."

"And ultimately that shiny trophy on the other side of the room."

Zim grinned. "That too."

"So, your father got you started, and then you moved here to Philadelphia."

"Yeah, where I joined a ten-and-under league."

Suji's eyes went wide. "They have a league for kids that young?"

"Younger. It's better to start very young. Though, at that age, it's more about getting the kids comfortable with being on the ice. Skating and stopping. Control. Falling."

"Falling?" Suji laughed.

"You fall a lot." Zim couldn't stop himself from smiling. "A whole hell of a lot until you're about sixteen when the skates and the stick feel more like extensions of your body."

"And now, here you are."

"Here I am."

"Well, if I didn't say it before, congratulations on winning."

Suji raised her glass and Zim followed suit.

"Thanks. And thank you for...accompanying me tonight."

"So far, so good," Suji said, her mouth curving in a grin.

"Very much so." Zim loved the blush that spread across her cheeks.

"There you are," Marty jogged up to the table. "We need you to make your speech, take some group shots, that sort of thing. Hi, Nurse Meriwether."

"Suji is fine," she offered. "And don't let me keep you, Zim. I know you have obligations."

He stood, hating the fact that they'd finally gotten to talk and he was being pulled away.

"I'll be as quick as I can," he assured her.

She waved him off. "Go make money for my kids."

Zim smiled. "That's the plan."

CHAPTER 11

SUJI STOOD near the back of the room to watch the introductions and speeches. She wasn't a big fan of these types of events, but couldn't deny that the turnout seemed promising. She recognized a few faces from the local elite. Politicians, entertainers, entrepreneurs. Hopefully, their checkbooks were open.

"Ladies and gentlemen," Calvin addressed the crowd, Zim at his side. "You all know why you're here tonight, to benefit the children of The Hospital of the University of Philadelphia, but you don't yet know the specifics of it. I'm joined by a local philanthropist and temporary owner of that beautiful trophy over there."

There was a light smattering of applause.

"Constantine Zimin is one of the most generous and humble young men I've ever had the pleasure of meeting. I admit, when he first approached us with the promise to help raise funds for our new Pediatrics wing, I was skeptical. But what I've learned of him, of the kind of person he is, I have no doubt that we'll do great things together. He recently shared some amazing news with me, and I invite him to share it with you. Zim?"

Zim stepped up to the microphone, looking decidedly uncomfortable in the spotlight. "Mama? Papa? Would you join me?"

His parents, surprised, judging by the looks on their faces, walked over to where he stood. There was a large, flat board on a tripod next to him, covered with a cloth.

"When I was nine years old," he began, addressing those gathered. "My twin sister, Mila, was diagnosed with a rare form of bone cancer, Ewing Sarcoma."

Suji's hand went to her throat. Ewing was a devastating form of the disease, and her heart went out to the Zimin family. She watched as Mr. Zimin quietly put his arms around his wife.

"At the time, the only real successes with treating Ewing were happening here at THUP. So, my father packed us all up, and we moved to Philadelphia to seek treatment. Dr. Jakob Kohn and his staff's forward-thinking gave us seven more years with my sister. We are forever grateful for that."

The crowd applauded, with a murmur of hear-hears as Zim and his parents gathered themselves. Suji could see the toll the loss of his sister had had on the three of them, his mother in particular.

"This year marks the tenth anniversary of Mila's death," Zim continued, his voice tight, hands shaking. "And, in her memory, I'm announcing my foundation, Mila's Room."

Zim and Calvin each took a corner of the cloth draped over the display and pulled, revealing a pale purple sign with dark purple lettering. The words "Mila's Room" curved along the mane of an abstract horse of some kind. No, not a horse, a unicorn.

"Mila's Room will provide assistance to families who find it an unbearable, financial hardship to travel to THUP for treatment, and will also offer temporary housing to those who need it," Zim announced with obvious pride. "I've donated the $200,000 bonus I received for winning The Cup, and I will be donating a portion of my salary for as long as I am able to play the game. What I need from you tonight is your pledge to support this cause."

There was more applause as Zim relinquished the microphone to the President of the Board of Directors for THUP, Dr. Sheryl Newell.

"Thank you, Mr. Zimin, for choosing THUP for the pilot program of Mila's Room. We're sure our children and their families will want to thank you themselves, once they learn of this."

Suji tuned out the rest of the chatter as she watched Zim accept handshakes from attendees. The entire time, his parents stayed close, still shaken by the announcement. His mother kept covering her mouth with her hand. Her husband would whisper in her ear and then she'd nod.

Clearly anxious to get away, Zim turned to his parents and ushered them back toward their table. He glanced up and caught Suji's eye, nodding to indicate that she follow.

She did. How could she not? He was…this guy was…

Shit.

The lone butterfly that had stretched its wings in her stomach back at the hospital had returned. With about a hundred thousand of her friends.

"Zim," Suji breathed, unable to articulate her feelings.

He smiled. "Surprise."

"You're such a good boy, such a dear boy," his mother crooned, still near tears as she sat at the table.

"How long have you been planning this?" His father asked, just as moved.

Zim pulled a couple of chairs over to their table, holding one out for Suji. She felt like an intruder. "Maybe I should let you have some family time."

"Nonsense," Lilya Zimin stated. "You're practically family."

"Mama," Zim softly chided her before turning to Suji. "Please stay."

The request was quiet as he met her eyes.

Suji nodded once and sat.

Zim lowered into the chair beside her and took his mother's hand. "I'm sorry I kept the news from you. I just wanted it to be a surprise."

"We're not upset, Kolya," his father insisted. "It's wonderful, we think it's wonderful."

Zim's mother nodded, patting his cheek.

"He is the best son we ever could have wished for," she said as she turned her silver-gray eyes on Suji. "We miss our Mila every day, but Zim has always exceeded our expectations. He has such a big heart."

"Yes, he does," Suji agreed.

Zim turned to her, his expression inscrutable. Something had changed in the air between them over the last couple of hours. The glance became a look. The look, a stare. The stare, a monolog full of promises, both filthy and sweet. Something told Suji knew he could deliver it all.

"I think dinner is served," Lilya broke the silence, snapping the bubble of tension. "Why don't you two young people go back to your quiet corner and enjoy your meal in peace." She gave her son a smile the Suji couldn't read.

Zim nodded. "You'll enjoy the meal, I picked the menu with you in mind."

He clasped his father on the shoulder as he stood and then offered his hand to Suji.

She took it, finding his warm and sturdy. Rather than let her go, he entwined their fingers as he led her through the dining room.

The waiter appeared as soon as they sat down, sparing her any uncomfortable silence.

"I'll have the petite sirloin, medium" she informed him.

"The porterhouse for me, medium rare." Zim poured them both more wine.

"This really is an amazing thing that you're doing," Suji spoke before the silence stretched on too long.

"Thanks, but it's not all me."

"I know, but it's your initiative. Don't be too shy to take credit where credit is due."

Zim chuckled. "Shy? No. I just…dislike excess attention."

"I gathered."

"Enough about me, though," he said, leaning forward with his elbows on the table. "Tell me more about Sujarta Meriwether. Are you from Philly?"

"Born and raised. My father is as well. My mother is from Mumbai."

"I've always wanted to visit India," Zim confessed, much to Suji's surprise.

"You should. It's an experience. Beautiful country."

"And did you always want to go into nursing? You seem young for someone in your position."

"I just turned thirty."

"Oh," he laughed softly. "An older woman. I like it."

Suji gaped at him. "I'm older than you?"

"Not by much. When's your birthday?"

"September twenty-third."

"Only just turned, then," he smiled, raising his glass. "Happy belated birthday, Nurse Meriwether."

Suji held her glass up to his. "Cheers, thanks."

"I celebrated my twenty-seventh back in June," he offered. "I suppose winning The Cup was my present."

"So, I'm less than two years older."

"I'm not complaining," he teased, his voice dipping down into a different octave.

The sound of it sent shivers up Suji's spine.

"Are you all right?" Zim's brow knit with concern.

Suji nodded. "Yeah, I just need some water."

She took a sip from her glass and tried to get a grip on herself.

Suji couldn't deny her body's reaction to Constantine Zimin, but it was moving quickly past physical attraction and into unchartered territory.

She liked Zim.

He was kind, generous, polite, funny, and it didn't hurt that she want to lick him like an ice cream cone.

And maybe her face had telegraphed that last thought a little too clearly because Zim was definitely staring at her. At her mouth, specifically.

She licked her lips to test the theory and, sure enough, he swallowed. Hard.

Luckily, the food arrived. During the meal, the conversation turned to the logistics of setting up a charity and rounded back to Suji's career in nursing.

"You just woke up one day and decided this was what you wanted to do?"

"Essentially," she replied as the waiter brought dessert, a decadent portion of tiramisu with two spoons. How romantic.

They'd polished off a bottle of red and were working on their second.

"My best friend got sick when I was in the second grade," Suji offered. "I remember visiting her in the hospital on the weekends, so upset that there was nothing I could do to help her. Her nurse had been amazing, though. She was a large woman with a cloud of white hair on her head. I used to think she was Mrs. Claus."

Zim laughed.

Suji smiled. It was a nice laugh. "After she recovered, I kept going back to the hospital to visit other sick kids."

"Really?"

"Is that strange?"

"No." Zim slowly shook his head. "I could see you doing just that."

CHAPTER 12

ZIM HAD A PROBLEM.

He was scheduled to return to training camp in just a few days and, for the first time in his career, he was not looking forward to it. This woman.

This woman.

"Am I that easy to read?"

Zim cleared his throat. "Sorry, what?"

He grabbed a spoon and offered it to her, taking one for himself. Zim waited until she took the first bite, enjoying the way her eyes rolled back into her head and the soft, little moan that escaped her throat.

Christ.

"My sister teases me about being so focused on the hospital, but it's who I am. I am a pediatric nurse."

"It's admirable, but it isn't all you are, Suji."

"No? And hockey isn't all you are?" She challenged him. "You're all about your training and your team, so tell me. How are we so different?"

She had him there.

"I think," he hedged. "Well, I'm learning that we don't have to be one thing and nothing else. I love hockey, but..."

"But?" She leaned forward, one arm on the table and the other hovering over the plate between them.

"My best friend, Jonas..."

"Is he a teammate?"

"Yes, or was. He just retired," Zim explained. "He got injured pretty badly during the Cup finals."

"Oh," her brow crinkled. He wanted to reach across the table and smooth it out. "Is he all right now?"

"Yeah, he's okay. Almost completely recovered. But it took that incident to make him see there was more to life than what we do for a living. He'd left someone behind, and now he's with her again. And he's happy."

"And you're thinking *why not me?*"

Zim shrugged. "I'm wondering what the heck I've been doing with my life, other than hockey."

"Well, I think you've done something wonderful today." Suji smiled softly.

"Thanks for that. But…do you know what I mean?"

"You want more."

"Which sounds selfish as fuck, pardon my language, but really. Who am I to want more of anything? I make an obscene amount of money doing something that I love. Sure, the hours suck, the travel is a bitch, and I rarely get to spend time at home, but I wouldn't trade it for anything."

"I know what you mean," Suji agreed. "I love my work, love the kids, love the crazy hours, even. I wouldn't give it up for anything or anyone."

"And you shouldn't."

"Neither should you," Suji insisted.

Zim laughed. "It's almost as if we share a brain."

Her smile was luminous as she stared down at the plate. "I guess we're bound to fall in love."

Suji's words were so matter-of-fact that Zim almost missed them. He thanked the stars he'd already swallowed his bite of tiramisu, or he definitely would have choked on it.

"Is that so?" He watched her drag her own tiny, silver spoon through the frothy cream.

Suji nodded, her eyes focused on the rapidly dwindling dessert between them.

"I think it is." There was a relaxed drawl to her speech, no doubt the result of the wine. "Can't you tell?"

He could. Of course, he could, though how he didn't know. It wasn't as if he'd ever been in this situation before, when the woman sitting across from him felt like she'd always been there. Felt, somehow, like home.

It was too soon to even think such things. Wasn't it? Not that he'd know.

"I'm not going to argue."

Her laugh was a husky, groan-inducing thing. "That would be a first."

Zim didn't know Sujarta Meriwether, not yet. Not really. Certainly not the way he wanted to, but he could tell. Suji was...something. If pressed against the boards, he still couldn't explain the how or the why, he just accepted the truth of it.

Even a blind man knows when the sun is shining.

A gorgeous, teasing grin spread across her kissable mouth and - BAM! Yeah, she was right. Of course, she was right, how could it go any other way?

"So how do we run this play?" Zim nudged her hand out of the way to claim his next bite.

Suji exhaled a soft sigh and capitulated, bringing her spoon up to a pink tongue that shorted out the circuits in Zim's brain when she licked at the curved surface.

"Well, normally, we would date a while, then maybe move in together, and then..." She flicked her eyes up to his.

"And then?"

Suji held his gaze for a long breath. In. Out. A smile curved her luscious lips, and then she went back to toying with their dessert.

"Let's not get ahead of ourselves," she said. "We haven't even had a proper first kiss, now that we actually know each other." Again, her gaze met his.

Suji Meriwether was a stunner of a woman. Cute as a button. Sexy as fuck. But this side of her, the side she showed him now – this playful, teasing, confident woman – he was instantly hooked.

At that moment, he pictured her at forty-five, standing beside him as they saw their first child off to college. At that moment, he saw them celebrating her sixtieth birthday with family and friends. At that moment, he had to act. He just had to.

Slowly, he put down his spoon, picked up his napkin, wiped his mouth, and then stood. Suji's gaze remained in his the entire time. He extended his hand, and she took it, dropping her utensil to the table as she rose. Zim guided her out of the dining room and onto the deck of the ship.

The late-summer breeze lifted the twists of chestnut hair that brushed her collar and Zim gathered them in one hand, using his other to gently circle her waist.

She gasped. A small, soft sound that did crazy things to his libido.

"Say yes," he demanded in as calm a voice as he could manage, which wasn't very.

Suji reached up, slid her hands into his hair and yanked his head down to hers.

Zim only had a second to breathe before she sealed her lips over his and his heart took off on a breakaway. He tightened his grip, pulling her closer. She tasted sweet, like cake and coffee and cream. He swept his tongue along hers, and she shivered.

When they came up for air, Suji took a long, slow breath. She slid her hands down his neck to his shoulders, gripping them tight before she opened her eyes and met his.

"Yes," she breathed. "Whatever it is, it's a yes."

CHAPTER 13

SUJI HADN'T EXPECTED their next stop to be a skating rink.

When she'd issued that breathy yes, after the best kiss she'd had in, well, ever, she thought they'd find the closest flat surface and quench the hunger that had been growing in her belly since she first laid eyes on him at the pub.

But, no. They were in an indoor ice rink with a handful of sweaty teenagers, Mr. Motz, his two bodyguards, and The Cup. Can't forget The Cup.

Worse yet, she wasn't exactly dressed for the frigid, ice-side temps.

"Cold?" Zim shucked his jacket and slipped it over her shoulders, planting a kiss on her temple. The smile he gave her was more intimate than it should have been, considering they'd only known one another for approximately forty-eight hours.

And she'd been ready to hop into bed with him. Twice.

What on earth had she been thinking?

Only now, with his warmth and his scent surrounding her, Suji found it damned hard to put up a fight. It was going to happen between them. No longer a question of *if*, but *when*.

When indeed.

"Keep your head up, eyes on the opponent," Zim yelled to one of the gangly kids on the ice.

"What opponent?" The kid yelled back.

"Use your imagination."

The kid, Beck, skated over to where they stood.

Suji realized he was older than she'd first thought. His babyface and wide-eyed adoration of Zim had stripped a few years of his age. Instead of sixteen or seventeen, he had to be closer to twenty.

"Time my sprints," the six-foot-gazillion-inches of gangly limbs and protective padding demanded.

Zim nodded. "Sure."

"And if I come in under ten seconds, you'll let me see it?"

"It's a deal, now hustle."

"Does he play too?" Suji asked, watching the younger man glide effortlessly across the ice. "Professionally, I mean."

Zim nodded. "He's in a minor league, but he has a chance at a farm team. I've been working with him this summer."

"How do you know each other? Or do all hockey players know one another."

Zim laughed, the rich timbre of his voice hitting Suji in all the best places. "We don't all know each other, though I know quite a few. Beck's family owns the house down the street from me. He house-sits for me while I'm out of town, or used to." He scratched his chin. "Suppose I'll need to sort out a new solution, once he gets picked up."

Beck skated off and somehow managed to look graceful doing it. He stopped at a blue line painted under the ice and turned back to Zim.

"Count down from three."

Zim set the stopwatch in his hand to zero. "In three…two…one… Go!"

The kid had a gift. He moved in a blur down the ice and back so fast that Suji felt a breeze from it.

"Wow."

"Right?" Zim's voice dripped with pride. "Nine-point-eight-nine."

"Shall I do the honors?" Mr. Motz gestured toward the black case that held hockey's most coveted trophy. He hadn't even finished unlocking it before Beck skated over, stripping off his helmet and gloves on the way.

"You ready to get as close to The Cup as you ever will?" Zim teased the boy, but Suji could tell how proud he was and wondered just how close the two were. There was a big-brother-little-brother vibe to their interaction.

She had no trouble seeing Zim as a mentor to the young player.

"Yeah," Beck retorted, still panting and trying not to smile. "And I promise I won't touch it."

"Hey, it's up to you," Zim replied.

Beck squinted. "But it's bad luck, right?"

"To some people, yeah, but there's no written rule."

Beck seemed to ponder that.

Jeff and Tony laid the case flat on one of the benches while Mr. Motz donned a pair of white gloves.

Suji peered over his shoulder. "Do you always wear those when you touch it?"

Motz nodded. "Yep, sure do."

"But you don't make anyone else wear gloves when they do."

"In more formal occasions, no one would touch it. It would be nice and shiny for photos," he said, as if it were something he said often. "I'm responsible for polishing The Cup after others have touched it, etcetera. It's easy to discretely get rid of a smudge when I'm wearing these." He held up his hands.

"Ah, gotcha."

Suji stepped out of the way as Beck clamored over the half wall and tentatively approached. Motz stood The Cup upright and stepped back to give the kid space.

Up close, Beck was huge. On skates, it was hard to tell how tall he was, but, with them, he easily matched Zim's height, though not his bulk.

She felt a hand close on her waist and found herself leaning into the touch. A warm breath ghosted over her ear.

"Hey, you."

Suji smiled but kept her eyes on Beck and Motz. "Hey."

Zim pulled her into the curve of his body, something that felt far more right than it should.

"Thanks for letting me make this pit stop."

"Are we going somewhere after this?"

Zim buried his nose in her hair and inhaled, sending goose bumps racing across her skin.

"I confess, I'm a bit out of my depths here," he muttered into the skin of her nape.

Suji found it hard to concentrate on anything at that moment. She just wanted more of him, wanted to be closer.

"Are you not a ladies man, Mr. Zimin?"

He chuckled. "Not in the least."

Suji turned her head to look at him. "Why is that?"

His gaze was locked onto her mouth, and Suji tortured him by licking her lips. Zim's full-throated groan was satisfying.

She decided to put him out of his misery, leaned up, and gently brushed her mouth over his.

Zim's tongue swept lightly across her bottom lip, and Suji felt the pull of it in her core. Her knees started to buckle, but she caught herself. Not before Zim noticed, though. When she met his eyes again, the raw hunger in them startled her.

"I have to leave for training in a few days."

She nodded. "I figured as much."

"I could take you home after this if that's what you want."

Despite his words, his arms came up around hers, and he pulled her into an embrace, her back to his front. Despite his words, Suji could feel the hard length of him pressing against her ass. Despite his words, this was going to happen.

"That's not what I want," she whispered into their bubble of intimacy.

Zim brought his head down to meet her eyes. "No?"

Suji shook her head, her gaze in his. "No."

"That's good, Nurse Meriwether," he said, his sinful mouth curving into a sly smile. "That's very good."

CHAPTER 14

ZIM COULDN'T REMEMBER the last time he'd wanted someone this fucking much. It had snuck up on him, somehow, this gnawing hunger that made his hands shake.

He'd met a pretty girl at a bar. Then met her again in an entirely different setting.

She'd impressed him with her passion for her work, had placed an unearned trust in him that he'd do right by her patients and the hospital. All very well and good.

But no one should look as sexy as she did in multi-colored scrubs, and she'd shown up to tonight's function looking good enough to eat. Zim was suddenly starving.

Still, he played it cool.

Until they walked through his front door.

The first to go was his jacket, which Suji let slide from her shoulders when he leaned in for the first of many kisses. Her tongue met his eagerly, the kiss turning frantic in milliseconds.

Zim drank from her mouth, slid his hands down over the soft fabric that covered her ass and cupped her through it.

She gasped into his mouth. "Jesus."

Zim broke the kiss. "Suji, I need to know what you want, because…"

She didn't let him finish that sentence. Her hands slid into his hair, the fingers pulling almost to the point of pain. One leg hooked over his hip as she lifted her mouth to his.

Zim took the hint, lifting her into his arms.

Suji's legs went around his waist, the heat of her core tantalizingly close to his burgeoning erection.

His cock pulsed, leaking already and pushing painfully against the zipper of his fly. Zim stumbled toward the stairs. He needed to get her upstairs to bed. He needed a wide, flat surface to do all the things he wanted to do to her.

They made it up three steps, kissing and clawing, before he lost his footing and fell back onto the steps, Suji atop him. The impact broke the kiss.

"Oh my God, are you okay?" She panted above him, hair disheveled, lips swollen and stripped of the lipstick she'd worn.

God, she was gorgeous.

"I'm fine," he managed to croak. "Come here."

Suji lowered her head as she centered herself across his lap. The feel of her pressed up against him drove him out of his goddamned mind, especially when she started to move against him.

"Oh, fuck."

"Yes, please."

The hard, wooden step digging into his back didn't matter. The fact that he was about to ruin a perfectly good suit didn't matter. Nothing mattered but the woman in his arms, and Zim shifted underneath her to give her what she wanted.

Suji moaned when the length of his cock hit just the right spot between her legs. Her breath caught, and Zim thought he might stop breathing altogether.

"I can't...I can't wait..."

"Don't," he commanded, thrusting against her. Despite the warning pulses of his own impending orgasm, Zim didn't relent. He grabbed her ass with both hands to aid her as she rocked.

And rocked.

And rocked.

"Oh, Jesus," came her breathy exclamation before she shuddered violently in his arms. "Zim...fuck."

"Yeah, yes, yes."

A sweet, mouthwatering scent filled his nostrils and Zim surged to his feet, careful to keep her in his arms. Through sheer willpower, he managed to make it to the master bedroom where he promptly dumped her onto the mattress.

Suji was boneless, spread out before him like a buffet. She stared up at him with half-lidded eyes and a satisfied grin.

Zim ran his hands down her sides to her legs, where he cupped her thighs and pulled them apart. They opened easily.

"I need to taste you."

"Yes," she replied.

Zim hooked his thumbs over the thin, elastic sides of her panties and drew them down, pushing the bottom of the dress up after he'd discarded them.

The sight of her, bare and perfect before him, shorted out his brain and sent even more blood rushing to his already painful erection. He lowered his head to her slick, quivering flesh and inhaled.

"You smell like heaven," he whispered, popping the button on his pants and lowering the zipper for a little relief.

Suji squirmed. Just a little twist of her hips.

Zim attacked her like a starving man.

"Oh, God!" Her voice was music to his ears.

Her hands grabbed onto his hair as he licked and sucked, nibbled and devoured her. She tasted like tart cherries and salted caramel and he was going to lose it. Come in his pants like a teenaged boy.

"I'm going to…you're going to make me…"

"Yes," he growled against her slick skin. "Do it. Come again for me, Suji. Fucking…just…"

"Wait…wait…" She jerked away, leaving him stunned.

"What's wrong?" Zim looked up to find her pulling the dress over her head.

"Tell me you have something because I need you inside me." She tossed the dress to the floor.

It took a moment for Zim's brain to come back online. "I, uh…yeah…"

He dove for the nightstand and wrenched open the drawer. The unopened box of condoms brought a sigh of relief from the beautiful, naked woman behind him as he toed off his shoes.

She plucked the box out of his hand, tossed it on the bed, and then went to work on the buttons of his shirt. She was being careful. Too careful.

Zim grabbed the two halves of the shirt and pulled. Buttons flew everywhere, and Suji giggled, her hands already pushing his trousers down. He had an overwhelming fear that she would touch him, stroke his throbbing, aching, dribbling cock, and all of this would be over in a flash.

He grabbed her face and crushed his mouth down over hers. The effect was immediate and she gripped his wrists, opening her mouth to his invasion while he stepped out of his pants and kicked them away. Zim lifted Suji by the waist and deposited her back on the bed before stripping off his boxer-briefs.

The way her eyes went wide as she took in the sight of him filled Zim with pure, male pride.

"Wow," she breathed, grinning.

Full breasts, full hips, a trim waist, and a softly curved belly, Sujarta Meriwether was all woman. Spread out beneath him like a goddess, he wanted to worship her.

"I could say the same," he said, climbing over her.

"Yeah?"

The uncertainty in her voice brought him up short. Zim paused to look into her eyes.

"Tell me you know how gorgeous you are." He straddled her hips and reached for the box of condoms.

Suji shrugged one shoulder. "I know I have…a certain appeal."

Zim chuckled. "A certain appeal?"

He tore open the box and fished out a strip of plastic squares, tearing one off. He ripped the packet open and removed the contents.

"This?" He circled one hand around his erection. "I've been like this for two days straight. Because of you."

Zim placed the condom on his leaking tip and slowly rolled it down, enjoying the bit of friction as well as the hungry look in Suji's eyes as she followed his hand.

"Promise me I can get my mouth around that before you go back to New Orleans," she practically moaned.

Zim had to grab the base of his cock and squeeze to keep from losing it right then and there.

"You," he started, once he could breathe again. "You cannot say shit like that to me right now."

Suji's laugh was sexy. "Promise me."

She reached down and took him in hand.

"Oh...*fuck.*"

"Promise." She guided him to her center and teased him by dragging the head up and down her slick cleft.

The heat of her, the scent. The sight of her spread out underneath him...in his bed...looking at him like he was all she ever wanted, it unlocked a door inside Zim he hadn't opened in a long, long time.

"Suji..."

"Now, Zim." She brought her legs up and around his hips, arching her back. "Now, please....now."

Zim slid home, and home is exactly what she felt like as her arms went around him. He buried himself in her depths, buried his head in the crook of her neck, and unearthed his long-dormant heart.

This was the start of something. This, right here, it was a beginning.

"So good," she moaned as he rolled his hips to meet hers. "God...Zim..."

Zim slid one hand up into her hair, bracing himself on the bed with the other. She looked amazing. Perfect.

"So fucking good," he agreed, fighting to go slow. To take his time. It was an impossible feat as Suji stretched up and ran her tongue across his open mouth.

He kissed her. It was hot and sweet, and they rocked together, perfectly in sync as if they'd done this a million times before. Zim felt her tighten around him, her body claiming his, and he surrendered.

"Baby..."

"Zim..."

He felt her shudder, heard the needy little whimpers followed by her cry of release, and he continued to rock into her. Relentless. Wringing out every bit of her pleasure he could before he lost his own battle with bliss. He bent to take a dark, puckered nipple into his mouth and her answering moan resonated right down to his balls.

His climax hit him like a freight train, slamming into his back and skittering up his spine, tightening the muscles in his legs and stomach. Zim couldn't breathe, the pleasure was so intense, so unexpected.

In the distance, he heard Suji's voice coaxing him on as he spilled into the condom. Into her.

Even the aftershocks were brutal. Zim's arms shook as he fell to his side. He grabbed a tissue to discard the condom and then gathered Suji into his arms.

"Wow." She draped one leg over his thigh and threw one arm across his stomach, resting her head on his shoulder.

Zim exhaled a laugh. "I second that."

He trailed one hand through her hair, across her shoulder, down her arm and back. Over and over, in an attempt to wrap his head around this. Around her.

"I have an idea," she said.

"Already? I need a few minutes." That earned him a playful slap on his belly.

Suji sat up. "You have something I can borrow? A shirt?"

His mind immediately latched onto the possibility of seeing her in his jersey and nothing else. Before he could talk himself out of it, he jumped up and grabbed one from his closet, holding it out to her with a flourish.

"Of course," she chuckled. "I should have known."

She put it on, and Zim was semi-hard again. Just. Like. That.

Suji tossed him his underwear. "Put these on and follow me."

Zim did as he as told.

They ended up in the living room, and Zim watched as she walked over to the black, flight case that held The Cup.

Fuck, he'd completely forgotten it was there.

"I think you should spend some time with it," Suji said, her voice barely above a whisper as she unbuckled the latches. "If you don't mind me being here with you, I'd like to stay."

Was she kidding? "You really think I'd let you walk out that door right now?"

He would, of course, if that's what she wanted. But fuck if he didn't want her to stay all night. And all day tomorrow. And the day after that. It hit him then that he'd be back in New Orleans in a few days.

Suji tried to open the case on her own, but it really was a two-person job. Zim joined her, and soon they had The Cup on his coffee table. Zim sat on the sofa and pulled Suji into his lap.

They sat in silence for long minutes, the only sound their mingling breaths.

"It really is amazing," she said, staring at the polished silver. "You don't like to brag, I've learned this about you already, but you've done something that few in your sport ever achieve. Be proud of that, proud of all the hard work you did to get here."

Suji turned in his arms and Zim slid a hand up into her hair to cradle her head.

He caught her gaze. Held it. Cherished it.

"You are so goddamned beautiful."

She blushed, then leaned forward and brushed a sweet kiss across his lips before whispering. "So are you, Constantine Zimin."

Yeah. He was done for. The question was, now what?

"This isn't going to be easy," Suji said, tracing a fingertip across his eyebrows.

"So, we're on the same page?"

She met his gaze.

"I think it's safe to say we are," she answered, a tinge of sorrow in her voice that he hated to hear.

Zim's hand tightened in her hair. "I want to make this work. Tell me how."

She shrugged. "I don't know, I guess we just...take it one day at a time? How often are you home?"

He winced.

"So." She smiled. "Not often."

"We play eighty-two games, not including the playoffs."

There was no way to sugarcoat the truth. He'd rarely be in Philly during the season. The Rage had only faced the Orange and Black twice last year.

"Look at your face," she said, smiling. "Zim, it's not a deal-breaker. I'm just trying to figure out what I've gotten myself into, here."

"You can still walk away."

Suji shook her head and ran a hand through his hair. Zim was sure it looked like hell.

"No, I don't think I can."

Well, shit. This was…it was fast. But Zim couldn't deny the fact that he was right there with her in it, whatever it was.

"Yeah," he croaked, pulling her up and over to straddle his thighs. "Me neither."

"So," she started, pecking him softly on the lips. "We take it a little at a time. If we need to make a decision later, we'll deal with it then. Right now, I just…I want to get to know you."

"Yeah?"

"Yeah."

"I wasn't expecting this, didn't expect you." Zim could hear the tremor in his voice. "But, damn, if you're in, I'm in."

"I'm in." Her smile flipped his world upside down.

Zim stood up, with Suji still wrapped around him, and headed toward the stairs. "Good, now let me in you again."

Suji laughed, warm and husky in his ear. "So cheesy."

"Get used to it," he teased.

"I plan to."

CHAPTER 15

SUJI AWOKE to strong arms around her body and soft kisses on her shoulder. She could get used to this but knew she shouldn't. At best, she'd only get a few days with Zim over the course of the hockey season, if they were going to move forward with this. And it looked like they were.

Wait, did that mean he was now her...boyfriend?

Holy. Shit. She wasn't ready for *that* conversation.

"Good morning." The deep, raspy rumble of his voice sent shivers across her skin and tightened her nipples. "Hungry?"

He had no idea. Suji was ready to push him down and ride him like a stallion, and then she remembered she had to go to work. And he had stuff to do as well if she recalled correctly.

"I could eat."

Zim chuckled. "I'll make us a quick breakfast, I know you need to get to the hospital. I can drop you off at your place on my way to meet Motz."

"The Cup goes back today?"

He nodded. "Yeah, and if I'm late, Motz will have my head."

"I don't doubt it."

"I was thinking," he said, pulling her until she lay flat on her back. Zim braced himself over her, leaning on one arm.

"Yes?" Suji couldn't help but smile up at him. He was damned sexy in the morning, the sunlight from the window revealing streaks of auburn in his hair.

"I could fly you out to games, when we're on the East coast, or even in the Midwest."

"I can fly myself."

Zim nodded quickly. "Yes, I know, but...well, you know what I mean. I just want to see you more than every other month."

"You're home in the summer, right?"

He nuzzled her neck. "Still wouldn't be enough. I'm addicted."

Suji giggled, a sound she didn't even know she could make. "Is that so?"

"Mmmm," he growled into her skin, lowering himself over her.

The weight of his body was delicious, and when he kissed her, Suji's heart tripped into a sprint. Damn. She was in so much trouble.

Smiling, she pushed at his shoulders. "Food. Work. Cup."

"Right," he said groaning as he rolled off her. "Coffee and a bagel?"

"Sounds perfect."

Suji watched as a very naked, yummilicious Zim crawled to his feet, his muscles long and lean. She wanted to pinch herself. The guy was sweet, kind, sexy, generous, loved his mom, was built like a tank, and looked at her like she was the sexiest woman on earth.

There had to be something wrong with him.

"What's wrong with you?"

Zim stopped in the doorway. "Huh?"

Suji eyed him as he threw on a pair of sweatpants. "There's got to be something wrong with you."

His grin was wicked. "Oh, baby. There's a lot wrong with me, but you'll have fun figuring it out. I promise."

She watched him leave the room, laughing. Grabbing his jersey from the floor, she slipped it on and followed him downstairs.

Oh yeah, she could get used to this.

CHAPTER 16

ZIM CAUGHT himself whistling along to Lady Gaga as he pulled up in front of Eddie's hotel. He shook his head.

"Jesus."

His phone pinged, signaling a message.

Motz: Checking out, will be out shortly.

Zim killed the engine, the smile he'd woken up with still plastered to his face.

Sujarta Meriwether. In just a few days, the woman had rocked his world, in more ways than one. He really liked her and knew it could quickly grow into a whole hell of a lot more if he weren't careful. The question was, did he want to be careful? And the answer to that was an emphatic *fuck no*.

She was a one-in-a-million kind of girl, and he'd fight to keep her. Fight to see where they could go.

His phone rang. Not Motz this time.

"Hey, asshole."

"Dude, congrats!" It was always great to hear from Jonas, but Zim hadn't been expecting to so soon.

"Uh, thanks?"

"Why didn't you say anything? Worried I'd be jealous?"

"Mags, it just happened. And how the hell did you find out, anyway?"

Jonas laughed. "Are you kidding? It's all over the trades. Five million dollars? That's amazing, man."

Zim sat up straight, his buzz from being with Suji all but forgotten. "Jonas, slow down and tell me what the fuck you're talking about."

"I'll read it, hang on." There was a rustling sound, and then Zim heard the keys of his computer clicking away. "Right, so it says *Constantine Zimin inks Five-million-dollar deal with MacroMuscle and launches a foundation to help sick children and their families.* There are some pics of you with some guys in suits, and one of you with one of the kids."

"What?"

"Yeah, taken yesterday. Looks like you're getting a lot of exposure for the foundation. It's Mila's, right? I bet donations will pour in. So happy for you, man."

Fuck. Fuckity fuck!

"Mags, hang on." Zim placed the call on speaker and opened a browser on his phone. It didn't take long for him to find the articles.

"Fuck me."

"Hey, what's wrong?" All signs of mirth vanished from Jonas's voice. "Zim?"

"So much, I don't know where to fucking start." Well, he knew where to start. Marty.

"Tell me what's going on."

"First, I didn't sign that deal yet. Marty just brought it to me yesterday, and I said I'd think about it."

"Then how did the press get a hold of it?"

"Exactly. Fuck if I know, but I can guess," Zim fumed.

"Marty wouldn't do that to you," Jonas tried to reason.

Zim couldn't say he was wrong. He'd been with Marty a long time, and the guy had never betrayed him.

He opened the rear gate when he saw Motz and the bellman wheel out his suitcase.

"I'll talk to him, but that's not my biggest problem."

The kid in the photo was little Aaron. Suji was going to have his balls for this.

The back gate closed, and then there was a rap on the passenger door. Zim turned to see Eddie standing on the other side. He unlocked it, and Motz opened the back door, tossing his carry-on inside before getting in the front seat.

"Zim, listen," Jonas said. "I know you don't like the wheeling and dealing part of this game, but this could help you raise money for Mila's Room. Help spread awareness, and stuff. You said you wanted to expand outside Philly, right?"

"Yeah, but not like this," Zim ran a rough hand over his face. "I just found her, I can't lose her like this."

Zim felt Eddie's eyes on him.

"Her who?" Jonas asked, clearly confused.

"I think Zim means Ms. Meriwether," Eddie so helpfully supplied. "She's a nurse at the hospital."

"Head Nurse in Pediatrics." Zim corrected the man without thinking.

"Hey Motz."

"Jonas." Eddie grinned. "So, Zim, I take it you had a good night."

"Whoa, whoa, whoa," Jonas interrupted. "Zimmer, you met someone? Since the last time we talked? Or were you hiding her from me?"

"Happened kinda fast," Zim admitted. "And it's probably over now, fuck."

"Wait, you said she's a nurse? At THUP?"

"Yeah, and that little guy in the photo is one of her patients."

Jonas groaned. "Oh, fuck. I take it the photo is unauthorized."

"May I see?" Eddie asked, and Zim turned the screen to him. "It looks like a private moment." He glanced up at Zim.

"He was kinda consoling me," Zim said, remembering how sweet the kid had been. "I thought I heard someone leave the room, but I didn't see or hear a camera. Marty told the reporters that the kids were off-limits unless the parents signed a release."

"Then, this photo is illegal," Eddie stated.

"Hell yeah, it is," Jonas agreed. "The parents can sue."

"Yeah, yeah. I know. But that won't matter, the damage has been done."

"Ms. Meriwether," Eddie said, pity in his voice. "I'm sure she'll understand, once you explain."

"Zimmer," Jonas drew his attention. "Listen, go see her. Explain. Get your attorney to send a cease-and-desist, whatever it takes. But first, go see your girl and explain. You don't want to leave town like this, not if you think you might have something real with her. I made that mistake."

"Yeah." Zim's stomach had fallen to his feet.

He knew what those kids meant to Suji. He had given his word - *his word* - that nothing like this would happen. Fuck.

"I need to take Eddie to the airport."

"I'll catch a later flight," the man said, surprising the hell out of him.

"Why?"

"Are you getting soft on us, Eddie?" Jonas teased, and Zim thought Eddie might actually be blushing.

"After a summer spent watching your entire team find love, it only seems fitting that Mr. Zimin has his own happily-ever-after."

"Yeah, let's not get ahead of ourselves." Zim started the car. "Mags, I'll call you later. I need to get Marty on the phone."

"Do it. And call me," Jonas demanded. "Good luck!"

He'd sure as hell need it.

***

He couldn't have known, she knew that. Suji had only met Constantine Zimin a few days ago, but she knew him well enough to know that he wouldn't have used Aaron like this.

Still, the irate phone calls from Aaron's parents weren't fun. Even Calvin cowered from their wrath. The board wasn't happy either. The hospital's security had been called into question, but Suji knew the board would look the other way in order to keep Mila's Room at THUP.

"Do you think he did it for the five mil?" Mimi shook her head, tsking. "That ain't right."

"No," Suji answered quickly. "I don't think he did it for the money. I don't think he did anything at all."

Mimi eyed her. "Is that you talking, or the afterglow?"

"I'm serious."

"So am I," Mimi countered. "Look, you called it. You said he'd use these kids to make himself look good, and look at this." She slapped the Inquirer down on the desk. "I was wrong, and you were right. I don't say that often, and I'm not happy to be saying it now."

"You weren't wrong," Suji argued. "I was. He is a good guy. I don't believe he did this. Let me see that again."

Suji picked up the paper. The photo of Zim with Aaron was actually really sweet. It tugged at the heartstrings and made him look like a caring guy, which he was. But to someone who didn't know him, it also looked opportunistic. It certainly had to Aaron's father, especially next to such a large sum of money.

She read the article, written by a name she didn't recognize. But then her gaze snagged on the credit under the photo itself.

Craig Bannon.

"Mother fucker."

Mimi raised her eyebrows. "So, you *do* think Mr. Hockey used us?"

"No." Suji turned the paper around to show Mimi. "Look at the by-line."

"Isn't that the jerk we had tossed out of here?"

"Yes, it is."

"Well, screw that. Dr. Morris should call the paper and get his credentials yanked."

"Yes," Suji agreed. "I'm sure he'll do more than that. Probably could get the police involved."

That explained the photo, Bannon was a sleaze. Still, Zim had exposed the kids to this. He may have had good intentions, but those often paved the way to hell.

Maybe it was a sign.

Things had moved quickly with them. He lived on the other side of the country, for Christ's sake. What had she been thinking?

"I suppose you were right about your boyfriend," Mimi said, nudging her.

"He's not my boyfriend."

"Oh no?" Mimi pointed over her shoulder. "You might want to tell him that, 'cause here he comes."

With that, she made herself scarce, leaving Suji to face the man who had turned her world upside down.

She had no idea what to say to him.

"Suji."

She turned. The look in his eyes, the panic, the terror, made her heart unfurl like a flower in the sun. Zim cared for her. A lot. It was written on his face in indelible ink. But could she do this?

"I know you didn't do anything wrong," she said and watched as he sagged with relief.

"I would never. Not ever."

"I know." She offered him a smile. "Come on, we need to talk."

Suji turned and walked toward one of the empty patient rooms. Zim followed. Once they were inside, she closed the door.

"Those are the scariest fucking words in the English language," he said before she turned back to face him. "Well, after *we think it's broken*."

Suji forced a smile.

"I am so sorry."

"I know, Zim, but…"

He cut her off. "Before you say anything else, just know that we had the photo pulled from the paper's website. We can't do anything about the print copies, but at least it won't be circulated online anymore. Not by the Inquirer. Any links pointing back to the article will re-cache without Aaron in it."

Suji nodded. "That's great, thanks for that."

"And my attorney is all over the paper for taking the pic without permission."

"We're handling it on our end too."

Zim nodded. "Is Aaron okay?"

Suji smiled. God, she really, really liked this guy. "He's okay. He has no idea what happened. His parents, on the other hand…"

"Shit." Zim ran a hand through his thick, brown hair. "If there are any damages, let me pay for them. I insist."

"They're not going to sue. But we did have to persuade them not to move him."

"Move him?" Zim snapped. "Aaron is getting the very best care here."

Suji nodded. "But he was exploited, in their eyes."

"Fuck."

"It's okay, Dr. Morris and I were able to reassure them. And he'll handle the board too."

Zim reached out and took her shoulders into his hands.

Suji stiffened, and he froze.

His hands dropped to his sides. "I am sorry."

"I know," Suji assured him. "But this just reminded me how different our lives are. Do you really think we could make a go of things, with you in Louisiana and me up here? With cameras following you everywhere, which is going to happen more now. Face it."

"I wish I could change things."

Suji shook her head. "But you shouldn't have to. You're a talented athlete, successful, you're doing something great for these kids. There's nothing you need to change."

"Suji," he stepped into her personal space and took her face into his hands, his thumbs brushing over her cheeks. "I've never…clicked with anyone like this. Not this fast and not this strongly. Fuck, I feel like…I want…"

He kissed her, and there was nothing ambiguous about it. He shook with his desire to make this happen, to make them happen, and she wanted to give in. Wanted to.

Suji returned the kiss, filling it with every emotion she felt. Passion, hope, doubt, resignation.

Zim pulled back. "You don't even want to try?"

Her eyes stung, but Suji swallowed the tears before they could fall.

"I think it's best if we leave it."

Suji watched the mask of acceptance settle over Zim's face before he nodded. "If that's what you want."

"I still want to work with you on Mila's Room."

He smiled. It was small, but it was there. Maybe they could be friends. Friends was good.

"I'd love that," he whispered.

"Okay then."

Zim stared at her, his eyes roaming over her face as if he needed to memorize it.

"Suji…"

"You're leaving soon, right?"

"In two days."

"Well, if I don't see you, have a safe flight and a great season."

He pressed his lips into a tight, thin line.

Suji didn't want to hear whatever he was trying not to say. "I should get back."

"Oh," he said, seeming to come back to life. "Right, yeah. I need to get Eddie to the airport."

Suji opened the door for him. "Say goodbye for me."

Zim stopped and turned to her. "How about I just say *see you later?*"

She nodded, losing the battle with her tear ducts. "That works too."

CHAPTER 17

"SO, that's it? You're just going to walk away?"

Zim had been sitting in his car for ten minutes listening to Eddie lecture him. Eddie Motz, of all people. Who knew he was such a hopeless romantic?

"What am I supposed to do, Eddie? Grab her by the hair and drag her back to my fucking cave? She doesn't want to pursue anything with me. I can't say I blame her. I mean, what could we really have anyway?"

Eddie shook his head. "Hockey players."

"What's that supposed to mean?"

"You're not the brightest bunch."

"Fuck you." Zim started the car.

Eddie reached over and turned it off.

"What the fuck are you doing?"

"No, Zimin. What the fuck are *you* doing?"

An angry Edward Motz was a sight. His lips thinned into non-existence and there was a definite twitch over his left eye. If Zim weren't so depressed, he would have found it funny.

"You made me miss my flight so you could go win this woman's heart, and you damn well better make it worth my while."

Zim sighed heavily. "What do you suggest I do?"

Eddie pointed out the window. "See that florist over there? Go buy it out. Every rose they have. Take it up to Ms. Meriwether's desk. Wow her. *Woo* her. She's into you, anyone with eyes could see that last night. Don't give up so damn easily. You're a Cup champion, for chrissake!"

Zim sat staring, his mouth hanging open. "Where did all of that come from?"

Eddie sighed. "Your team is one of the best bunch of guys I've ever had the pleasure of being around. Nice, upstanding men. And you know the one thing they all have in common?"

Zim shook his head.

"They all admire you." Eddie shrugged. "Flynn, Ransom, every single one of them looks up to you. And Jonas? Jonas thinks of you like a brother."

"Same," Zim answered without hesitation. "But what does any of that have to do with this?"

"What do you think they'd say if they knew you'd walked away from a chance with a woman you really like, and could even love one day, because of who you are and what you do, where you play?"

"That's not what…"

"Isn't it? You're letting your career, your notoriety, the distance between here and New Orleans – there are planes, by the way – get in the way of what you could have with Ms. Meriwether."

"It wasn't my choice."

"Ah, but did you even put up a fight?" Eddie gave him a knowing look.

Zim grunted. "Roses, eh?"

Eddie smiled. "Roses. Fill The Cup with them."

"What?"

"Come on, we don't have a lot of time. I need to be back in Toronto tonight."

With that, he got out of the SUV and Zim had no choice but to follow. He had no idea what had gotten into the Keeper, but if Eddie had ideas on how to win Suji back, he was all ears.

***

Suji dried her eyes for the umpteenth time. It was getting ridiculous, but she blamed Amrita. As soon as she texted her sister to tell her things with Zim didn't work out, she'd regretted it.

Of course, Amri was going to call. Of course, Amri was going to tell her she was being stupid. Of course, Amri would say she'd just made the biggest mistake of her life.

The problem was, Suji knew she was right. It had been a mistake to send Zim packing before they'd had a chance to figure out what they could be. And what they could have been was something. Because if she felt like this after only having known him for a couple of days, and having only spent one night in his bed, in his arms, the thought of losing what they could have been made her unbearably sad.

It was fear holding her back. Fear of failure, her failure. Theirs. She didn't want to invest in a relationship only to have it fall apart around her again. But that was fear talking.

Zim wasn't Brian. And she wasn't a coward.

Suji swooped past the nurse's station on the way to her office. "Mimi, I need to make a call. Grab me if you need me."

Mimi grinned. "Uh huh."

"What?"

"Oh, nothing."

Suji frowned but didn't stop. She had to catch Zim before he wrote her off entirely. She rounded the corner and opened the door to her office.

On her desk sat The Cup, filled with dozens of red and white roses.

Next to her desk, stood little Aaron.

Tiffany sat in Suji's chair, grinning like a Cheshire cat while her legs dangled above the floor.

"What's going on?" Suji stood in the doorway, her heart pounding like she just finished a marathon. "What are you two doing in here?"

"I asked Mimi to bring them."

Suji's knees turned to jelly at the sound of Zim's voice behind her. She gripped the doorknob tight.

Zim stepped around her and knelt before Aaron. "Hey, buddy."

"Hi, Subzero!"

"I just wanted to say I'm sorry to you and to Tiffany. I promised you a jersey, and I didn't give it to you yesterday. I hope you'll take this for now until I can get one over to you tomorrow."

Zim took something out of his pocket and put in the boy's hand.

Aaron gasped. "Is this…is this your Cup ring?"

Suji caught a glimpse of jewel-encrusted metal before Zim threaded a chain through it and placed it around Aaron's neck.

"Hold onto this for me until tomorrow, and I'll bring your jersey. Can you do that for me?"

"Yes!" Aaron nodded, clutching the ring to his chest.

"Don't lose it."

"I won't, I promise."

Suji had never seen the child so happy.

Zim stood and went around the desk. "And Tiff, I wanted to ask if you could help me with something."

"What?" She hopped out of the chair. "You have another ring?"

Zim chuckled. "No, but help Aaron keep an eye on that for me, would you?"

"Sure thing."

"Also, I'd love it if you could be my official stats keeper. For my website and stuff. Think you could do that?"

"Is it a paying job?"

"Of course."

Tiff nodded, scratching her chin as if she were thinking it over. "Yeah, I could do that. After I ask my parents."

"Of course," Zim agreed. "Ask first, then we'll talk."

"Deal." She stuck out her pinky and, to Suji's surprise, Zim took it with his own. They shook.

"Awesome. Now, could you two stand guard in the hall for a few minutes? I need to talk to Nurse Meriwether."

Aaron eyed him with suspicion. "Are you going to kiss her?"

"Aaron," Suji warned, trying not to smile.

Zim laughed out loud. "I sure hope so, buddy." He caught Suji's gaze. "If she'll let me, that is."

Tiffany took Aaron's hand and walked him to the door. Suji moved to let them through, and Tiff looked up at her.

"We'll be right outside if you need us."

"Thank you, Tiff. I appreciate it."

Tiff nodded and then they were gone.

Suji closed the door.

"Zim…"

She didn't have time to say anything else.

Zim gathered her in his arms and slanted his mouth over hers. It wasn't the bruising, frantic kisses they'd shared at the pub or even at his house. It wasn't the brain-melting kiss he'd given her at dinner or the soft, chaste goodbye he'd given her that morning when he dropped her off.

This kiss was full of unspoken promises.

His tongue swept between her parted lips, and Suji opened for him, surrendering. It lasted for long minutes before he finally broke away, breathing hard. His hands felt so good, holding her tight.

"I'm going to fight for you," he said, his voice ragged. "For us. Because I think this has the potential to be something. Maybe everything. I want to know every little thing about you. I want you to know me. I want us to find ways to be together, whether it's for five minutes or five hours, or five days. Please."

He ran a hand through her hair and searched her eyes.

"This can't end, Suji, not yet. Just…I don't want to walk away from this."

"Neither do I," she hastened to tell him.

He froze, his eyes wide.

"I was going to call," she continued. "I want this. With you. I want to see where it goes. Because…I…"

"Because?" The hope in his eyes gave her courage.

"It's never been like this for me either, not like this." She trailed her palm across his stubbled jaw. "Not like you. So, let's try. I want to try."

Zim smiled, exhaled, nodded. "Good, that's very good, Nurse Meriwether."

And yeah. It was.

"So," he started, his hands roaming into dangerous territory. "Any chance you can duck out of here early?"

Suji smiled up at Zim, and ran her fingers into his hair to scrape her nails across his scalp.

He rewarded her with a low groan.

"Did you have something in mind for this afternoon, Mr, Zimin?"

Zim pulled her tight against his front. He was hard. Everywhere.

"I just think it's best we get out of here. Now, unless you want to scar those poor kids out there for life."

EPILOGUE

THREE MONTHS LATER...

Zim never got nervous before a game, yet he found himself bouncing off the walls. Philly was a tough team, and he knew it would be a battle on the ice, but that wasn't the reason for his jitters.

"You all right, Connie?" Rage leftwinger Anders Sorensen gave him the once-over. "You look a little green. Worried about playing in front of your home crowd?"

"They'll boo, it's what they do," said Cooper Banks, another leftwinger. "It is Philly, after all."

"Some will boo, but some will cheer their hometown talent," Sorenson chimed in. "Coop's right, though. You do look shellshocked. Everything okay?"

"Yep." Zim waved them off.

"Hey, is this your first home game in front of your girl?" Leave it to Sorenson to zero in on the problem. Damn wingers and their damned sixth senses.

"Oh!" Coop exclaimed. "Will we finally get to meet this mystery woman?"

"That's up to her," Zim replied. "Anyway, my parents are here too."

"Aww." Anders grinned. "Mommy, daddy, and girly. We better play good, boys. Can't embarrass Connie in front of his family."

"Fuck off." Zim laughed despite himself. He did love these guys.

They won in overtime.

Local fans were none too happy, but they'd been respectful of Zim as one of their own. A few fans hung around after the game, and he was more than happy to sign autographs for them.

"Think you'll ever play for us, Subzero?" The kid who had asked was probably fourteen.

"I love my team, but never say never." Zim hoped his answer was sufficient. Judging by the boy's grin, it was just fine.

"That would certainly make things easier."

Zim looked up to find Suji smiling down at him, flanked by his mom and dad. And didn't that paint a pretty picture.

In the three months since they'd decided to see where things might go, they'd gone very, very well.

He'd flown home when he could, and she'd come down to New Orleans, or wherever he was playing when she could. It was far from ideal, but they were making it work.

Better yet, it had been so worth it. She was worth it, worth everything.

"What?"

Zim hadn't realized he was staring at her. "Nothing."

"Well, go get changed so we can have dinner." Suji winked. "Your dad is hungry."

"Starving," his father agreed.

"You just had a pretzel, and beer, Genya," his mother chided lovingly. "How are you already hungry?"

Zim's father laughed. "Watching these boys play, I felt like I was out there."

Lilya shook her head. "Boys never change."

She caught Zim's eye and winked.

"Come on, Genya, walk me to the restroom."

"You just went," his father complained but took her arm to help her up the steps.

After they had left, Zim reached up, and Suji slipped her hand into his notching their fingers together.

She looked fucking amazing in her fitted jersey, and he really liked seeing his last name on her. Her smile was radiant, and Zim's heart swelled to three times its size in his chest.

Fucking hell.

He loved this woman.

Suji leaned over the railing and Zim cupped her cheek before accepting her kiss. It seared the emotion into him.

When she pulled back, she didn't go very far.

"Hey," she whispered, smiling.

"Hey."

"Ever have sex in a locker room?"

Zim coughed, nearly choking on his own tongue. He looked around, grateful that the fans had moved on to one of his teammates.

"Christ, lady, you can't say stuff like that."

She grinned. "Have you?"

And now he was hard. Sweaty and hard, and still in his gear. "No."

Her grin was positively evil. "Wanna?"

She wiggled her eyebrows, her tongue peeking out to run along her imperfect white teeth.

Fuck yeah, he did.

"Get over here."

One leg over the railing, two, and then she was in his arms. Zim kissed her for everything he was worth as she wrapped her legs around his waist and he made his way down the tunnel.

He was gonna catch so much shit for this.

Ask him if he cared.

BONUS CHAPTER

"Traded?"

Zim sat back in the chair, his body hitting the hardwood with a resounding thump, and stared hard at the man across the desk from him.

Coach Rage opened his mouth to speak, but nothing emerged. He looked wounded.

"Traded." The word bounced around in Zim's head like a glass marble in a porcelain sink.

"Zim." Coach's tone was cautious. Conciliatory.

Meanwhile, Zim struggled not to erupt. "Fucking traded?"

"Hear us out before you blow a gasket." This from the other voice in the room.

Zim didn't even acknowledge the man sitting next to him. When Marty put his hand on Zim's arm, he couldn't help but stiffen. Out of the corner of his eye, he saw Marty flinch. He let out a slow breath.

"Okay. Right, sorry. I just…" Zim exhaled again. "Sorry."

"I get it," Coach said. "You mean a hell of a lot to this team, Zim. You always will. But so many of the guys from the Cup team are gone, and we need to rebuild."

"It's a good deal, Zim."

Zim turned to Marty. "How long have you known about it?"

Marty glanced nervously at Coach Rage. "I-I-I only learned about it five minutes before you did. I was on my way to see you."

"About what?"

"About the fundraiser for *Mila's Room Too*."

Zim's temperature, which had skyrocketed to the approximate temperature of the sun, dropped a few degrees. His shoulders sank.

"Oh."

"And when I saw Marty in the hall," Coach interjected. "I grabbed him and sent for you."

Wiping the sweat from his forehead with his sleeve, Zim resigned himself to the news. Getting traded wasn't a new thing to him. He'd been through it all before. But things had only just begun to feel settled, somewhat. He had a routine and had finally worked out how to see Suji on a semi-regular schedule. Who knew what fresh hell this would bring? He could end up in…wait.

"Is it Vancouver?"

Coach Rage frowned, clearly surprised. "How did you even hear about that?"

Taking that as confirmation, Zim shrugged and rose from his seat. Damn. "News travels. When do I leave?"

Vancouver. Fuck. It may as well be Mars. He loved the city, but he didn't love the additional 1800 miles it would put between him and Suji.

Coach Rage sat back and crossed his arms. "Today. But it's not Vancouver."

Zim froze. "Oh. Well, where?" He glanced at Marty.

The man was practically beaming.

"You were traded to Calgary for a young, hotshot center." Coach supplied instead. "Calgary traded you to Buffalo for a rookie goalie whose hands are like magnets. Calgary traded you to Philly for one of their winger prospects and a 2nd round pick in the draft."

"And who did Philly trade me to?" Zim didn't dare hope. But when Coach didn't respond, he turned to Marty.

"As soon as Philly found out you were available, they started calling around. They made this deal happen." Marty shrugged and gave him a half-grin.

Zim swiveled his head between the two men. If anyone had seen it without context, they'd think he were watching a tennis match.

The kernel of hope in his chest grew.

"Are you shitting me?"

"Nope." Coach stood and offered his hand, and Zim was so damned torn when they shook.

This was New Orleans. His team. His brothers were there, some anyway. Most of the cup-winning team had disbanded, but Zim was still a Ragin' Cajun, through and through.

But…

Philly was home.

Philly was mama, and papa, and homemade *olivie*. It was water ice and hoagies, Rocky and the Liberty Bell. It was running along the river and driving along The Drive.

It was Suji.

Her smile. Her laugh. Hell, even her fiery temper. Home. All of it.

The probability of what was about to happen threatened to turn Zim's knees to mashed potatoes, so he sat back down before he fell down. Life as he knew it was about to change and he was more than ready. In fact, he took it as a sign.

Zim looked back and forth between his agent and his coach. "Right, so, uh…I need a favor."

***

Showing up at hospital unannounced was risky, but Zim had taken precautions. As soon as he'd landed at Philadelphia International, he'd phoned the nurse's station and spoken to Mimi, confirming that Suji was still there and that her shift ended in an hour.

Next, he'd checked Twitter for any mention of the trade. Asking Coach to keep the news under wraps until morning was a lot to hope for, but so far so good.

Then he called his parents. After his mother had finished laugh-crying into the phone, his father asked him what he needed him to do. That was his dad. Always ready.

After the 'rents, Zim texted Beck.

ZIM: Are you home?

BECK: yeah whassup

ZIM: I need a huge favor.

BECK: what's in it for me

ZIM: What do you want, you little shit?

BECK: hostilities already [middle finger emoji]

ZIM: Beck.

BECK: finnnne what do you need? we can discuss payment later all-star

Hopefully, Beck had been able to get everything ready at the house. Zim had reservations about entrusting one of the most important days of his life to a party-happy college student, but desperate times and all. Besides, Beck had done a great job of keeping an eye on things while was out of town.

Zim stepped off the elevator and walked toward the brand new glass doors that served as the entrance to the renovated children's ward at THUP. He took a moment to run his fingertips over the plaque mounted to the right of the doors.

For Mila's Room

Turn right and follow the rainbow trail

That had been Suji's idea, turning the journey to the long-term family facilities into a magical adventure. Unicorns were painted on the walls of the hallway, and a trail of painted cobblestones led to the newly finished space. The entrance had an honest-to-goodness castle door, thick hardwood complete with a cast iron knocker. There wasn't a trace of the hospital once you entered the space. Cozy bedrooms, a shared communal living room, and a kitchen kitted out with stainless steel appliances, granite countertops, and warm, inviting furniture.

Suji had made it a home away from home for guests, and Zim had fallen a little more in love with her every time she updated him on the project.

Zim pushed through the glass doors, taking a moment to adjust to the now-familiar antiseptic smell, and made his way toward Suji's office.

"Zim!" Dr. Calvin Morris jogged to catch up, extending his hand. "I didn't know you were in town."

"The team is playing New York tomorrow, so…" He let the sentence hang as they shook hands.

It wasn't a lie, New Orleans was scheduled to play New York. He just wouldn't be on the ice with them. He'd be in Philly, dressed in orange and black, and facing Carolina.

"Ah, gotcha. Are you looking for Suji? I think she's in her office taking care of some paperwork."

"I am, thanks." Zim saluted as Calvin headed for the elevators.

"See you soon, SubZero."

"Well, if it isn't the prodigal son," Mimi cooed, grinning beneath her purple bifocals.

Zim liked her. She was one of those people that treated you like a life-long friend five minutes after meeting you, unless you gave her a reason not to. And she was a good friend to Suji, which put her on his 'trustworthy' list. She was the only other person he'd told about the trade.

"Heya, Mimi." He leaned across the desk and planted a soft kiss on her plump cheek, loving the blush that rose up in her skin. "She still back there?"

Mimi's grin gave birth to dimples. "Yep. Hurry, though. I think she's almost done and you don't want her to ruin your surprise."

"No ma'am." Zim grinned.

"By the way, welcome home."

Zim squeezed her hand as he passed. "Thanks."

The door was closed when he reached it, affording Zim a moment to steel his nerves. This would either go well for him or blow up in his face.

"Come in." Suji's voice always sent a little jolt of pleasure through him, but when she was in office mode, the jolt was around a thousand mega joules. Yeah, he had office fantasies about Suji. Could anyone blame him?

Zim pushed inside.

Suji sat at her desk, her head bent over a stack of papers as she scribbled furiously. Her scrubs were pink today, with what looked like carousel horses. Her hair was down already, a clear sign that her day was nearly done. It had grown in the last year, brushing the tops of her shoulders.

"Sorry, I'll be right with you."

"Take your time."

Her head snapped up at the sound of his voice.

Zim grinned at her shocked expression.

"Z."

"Hey." He shut the door, warming at the sound of her nickname for him.

She rose from her seat, papers forgotten, and circled the desk to meet him.

He already had his arms open, pulling her into a heated kiss the moment his fingers touched her.

Suji melted against him like ice cream in the noonday sun, and he loved it. Loved it. Loved her.

The kiss settled him. For the first time in weeks, he felt grounded again. This was what she did for him. Was to him. She was the earth beneath his feet.

Reluctantly, Zim released her soft, pillowy lips and planted one last kiss on her forehead.

Her grip on his waist was firm and sure. Suji had never had any issues in claiming him, something that was a source of pride.

Coal black eyes blinked up when he looked down.

"Hi." She smiled, her lips curving wickedly.

"Hello, yourself."

"This is a surprise."

"It was meant to be, though I know you're not a fan of them."

Suji's laugh was smoky. "Not generally, no, but yours have been all right. So far."

Zim arched an eyebrow. "So far, eh?"

"Mm-hmm." She stretched onto her toes, her chin tilted, silently asking for another kiss. Which he granted. Of course.

"Come home with me?"

Suji leaned back, eyeing him. "No romance today, huh? Straight to the point."

Zim's jaw dropped. And then he had to laugh, because, holy shit. This woman. He wrapped her up tight, raining kisses on her face and hair while she giggled.

"Not that I hadn't planned on ravishing you, but that's not the only reason I want you to come home with me."

Suji tilted her head back to look up at him. It seemed damned uncomfortable, so Zim loosened his hold on her.

"Oh? Should I be scared or worried?" She grinned, but he could see the real concern behind it.

"Neither." He gave her his patented mega-watt smile.

Suji extricated herself from him and went back to her desk. "Oh, now I am *really* worried."

She powered down her computer and grabbed the stack of papers she'd been signing. Slinging her bag over her shoulder, she walked back over to him.

"Alright, then. Let's go."

***

Leaving the prep to a twenty-year-old wasn't ideal, so Zim didn't really know what to expect when he turned the key to his brownstone, but they stepped into a fairytale. Zim mentally pumped his fist and made a note to get something special for Beck. He'd gone above and beyond.

There were candles. Everywhere. And roses, a few dozen, scattered in various clear, glass, vases. The candles were newly lit, and Zim wondered how Beck had gotten the timing just right. Then he heard the tell-tale click of the back door and chuckled to himself.

Behind him, Suji gasped.

He turned and found her slack-jawed, her gaze sweeping the living room.

"Z," she breathed. Her bag hung precariously from her fingertips. Zim gently took it and placed it on the wingback by the window.

Suji snapped out of her trance and looked at him with shining eyes. "What is this? What are you doing?"

She trembled, and Zim took mercy on her, pulling her into his arms as he sat down on the couch. She settled across his lap, but her gaze bounced around the room before it landed back on him.

"I want you to move in."

No point in beating around the bush.

Suji frowned. "In…here?"

"Your lease is up in three weeks, right?"

She nodded.

"And it doesn't make sense for you to find another rental when I have a perfectly good house here."

Her frown deepened. "You want to rent the house to me?"

What?

"What? No, Suji. I want you to move in *with* me."

Her expression remained unchanged.

Zim was suddenly nervous. "Bad idea? Am I doing this all wrong? It sounded good in my head."

She finally softened. Or sagged, if he were honest with himself. She visibly deflated. Whatever it was she'd been expecting, he'd not met her expectations.

And, yeah, he could probably guess what it looked like to her when they first walked in, but he'd been too chicken shit to even consider proposing. This. This was a big step. *That*, well…

"Suji, say something."

"I…" She swallowed, her eyes on her hands which sat fidgeting in her lap. "It's a very generous offer. Thanks. I'll…have to think about it."

Oh, fuck that.

"Suji."

She finally turned her face to him, and Zim felt like he'd been kicked in the gut. He'd really fucked this up.

"Baby."

Her eyes flashed with fire. "What? You thought I'd just move in here? Jump at the chance to live in your big, beautiful *empty* house? It's hard enough, you not being here much. You want me to live inside the one, constant reminder of just how not here you are?"

"About that…"

"I can't, Z. I…" She swallowed hard, and Zim's heart twisted.

He knew.

He knew how hard it was for her, despite her constant reassurances it was fine. That the distance was fine. That the travel was fine. That they were fine.

They were. Fine. But…

Zim maneuvered her until she straddled his thighs. Then he cupped her face in his hands and waited for her to meet his eyes. She seemed almost embarrassed by her longing. He needed to show her it was the same for him. Had always been just as hard on him. But first, he needed to fix this debacle.

"I'm in love with you, Suji."

She hiccuped, a tiny smile on her lips. "I'm in love with you too."

"And I hate every second that we're apart."

She nodded. "Yeah."

"You don't look like you believe me." He slipped one hand up into her hair. "Maybe I can convince you."

Zim didn't have to pull her in, Suji was right there. Her mouth on his, hot and hungry and desperate. It was lips and teeth and tongue. It was words unspoken for far too long. Zim broke the kiss, breathing hard.

"I fucking hate being away from you."

Eyes still closed, she nodded frantically. "Me too. So much."

"But I have news that will help."

"Yeah?" She blinked, meeting his gaze. Hers full of hope.

Zim dragged his thumb across her kiss-swollen bottom lip. God in heaven, she was the most beautiful woman he'd ever seen.

"I was traded."

Her eyebrows shot up. "Traded?"

He nodded. "To Philly."

Suji went still. "You…*What?*"

Zim hadn't expected the anger.

"Oh my fuck, Zim!" She slapped his arm. It stung. "Way to bury the lead."

He thought he'd fucked up. Again. But then she burst into bright, raucous laughter, shaking and holding her stomach.

He laughed too, mostly because seeing her like that was a rare treat. Suji was a lot of fun, but she rarely let go so completely.

"F-f-first," she said when she could catch her breath. "I thought you were proposing."

Damn.

"And then I thought you were trying to rent me this place out of some misguided sense of I don't know what. But then you wanted me to move in with you when you're never here, to begin with. Now you tell me you're going to play for Philadelphia? Since when?"

"Since this morning."

"I didn't hear anything about a trade."

"You will by morning. I asked Coach to hold off on accepting until then. I wanted time to...to..."

"To freak me out?"

Zim winced. "Sorry?"

Suji laughed again and wrapped her arms around his neck, burying her face there. He gladly, gratefully accepted the embrace, looping his arms around her and pulling her tight against him.

She fit. They fit. They always had, and he had a feeling they always would.

"I'm not moving in here," she mumbled into his skin.

Zim was too content to hold her. Her words didn't sink in right away. When they did, he pushed her back.

"What did you say?"

She arched one perfect eyebrow. "I said I'm not going to just move in with you."

"Why not?" It was the perfect solution. Couldn't she see that?

"Because it's not how this goes."

"No?"

She shrugged. "No. I'm not the type to just shack up."

Zim was about to argue that she'd lived with her ex, but decided that was probably not the best tactic. Besides, he could see her struggling not to laugh. She was yanking his chain.

"Oh. Alright, then. I can always ask Coach to work another deal." He offered an exaggerated sigh and ran a hand through his hair. It had also grown out. He wasn't a fan, but Suji loved it. And anything Suji wanted he'd lick the ice to give her.

"Don't. You. Dare." She said, eyeing him with enough heat to melt a glacier. Suji pecked him on the lips. "Of course I'm moving in. I told you when we first started all this that we would fall in love, then maybe move in together."

"And get married," he finished for her.

Her eyes widened. "Uh...yeah."

Zim studied her for a bit, this woman that had turned his life upside down from the first moment they'd met. This woman who had thawed his long-frozen heart. This woman.

He ran a hand through her thick, wavy hair. Smoothed it back from her glorious cheekbones.

"Do you want to?" His voice sounded small, even to him.

She tilted her head. "I already said I would. I'd love to live with you, Z."

"Not what I meant."

Her breath hitched. "Oh."

He held her gaze, watching the thoughts play out behind her beautiful, onyx eyes.

"Do you?" Her voice wobbled.

"Yes," he answered, without hesitation. "Yes, I do."

Her mouth curved into a smile. "Those words sound good coming from those lips."

Zim grinned. "Yeah?"

Suji nodded. "So, marry me then."

"Okay." His heart thundered in his chest, and he saw the answer to it in the ticking vein at the base of her throat.

"Okay." She smiled, sliding her palms up his jaw to hold him. "You're going to play for Philly. I'm moving in. And we're getting married."

"Just like that?" Zim slid his hands around to her ass and pulled her flush against him. She widened her thighs and wound her arms around his neck, bringing her lips tantalizingly close to his.

"Just like that."

ACKNOWLEDGMENTS

Huge thank yous go to Avery Flynn for inviting me to be a part of the *Hot On Ice* anthology and for keeping us all organized.

And to all of the other authors involved with *Hot On Ice*: Kimberly Kincaid, Susan Scott Shelley, Angi Morgan, Misty D. Waters, Christi Barth, Kim Golden, Kate Meader, Heather Long, Virginia Nelson, Robin Covington, Robin Kaye, Lena Hart, Desiree Holt, Andie J. Christopher, Katie Kenyhercz, and Nana Malone, thank you for making it such a fun, crazy experience!

ABOUT THE AUTHOR

Xio Axelrod is a USA Today bestselling author of love stories, contemporary romance and (what she likes to call) strange, twisted tales.

Xio grew up in the music industry and began recording at a young age. When she isn't writing stories, she can be found in the studio, writing songs, or performing on international stages (under a different, not-so-secret name). She lives in Philadelphia with one full-time husband and one part-time cat.

Where to find Xio...

Twitter: @xioaxelrod
Facebook: XioAxelrod
www.xioaxelrod.com
xio@xioaxelrod.com

ALSO BY XIO

Honourable Mention: 2016

Readers' Favorite Awards - Drama

Falling Stars (Book 1)

What if you met the right person at the absolute wrong time?

Meet Val Saunders and Sam Newman, two Hollywood actors at opposite ends of their careers. Hers is skyrocketing while his, well, never really took off. Fate brings them together when they're cast as lovers on a steamy new television series. The on-screen chemistry between them is off the charts and when it spills over into a real life attraction, they find themselves in a situation.

Winner: 4th Annual Swirl Awards

Best New Adult Romance

Honourable Mention:

2015 Readers' Favorite Awards

Contemporary Romance

The Calum

Twenty-six is too old to believe in fairytales, but tell that to Lovie's roommate. Convinced she'll find a real life version of her ultimate book boyfriend, Calum MacKenzie, Jo drags Lovie to the Scottish Highlands. Lovie's no cynic *ahem* but she knows The Calum is a myth. A construct. A freaking unicorn! And there are warmer places to spend a winter vacation.

www.ingramcontent.com/pod-product-compliance
Lightning Source LLC
Chambersburg PA
CBHW051956170626
46808CB00007B/2640